A MAZE OF MISCHIEF

Miss Isabel Garnett was a well-brought-up young lady posing as a lady's maid.

Even more deceiving, Miss Corliss Hewett was a young lady posing as a lady's maid posing as a lady.

But the most deceptive of all was handsome, wealthy, and aristocratic Colonel Douglas Renfrew, a gentleman who clearly had no heart—but whose heart had to be won by Corliss.

For the colonel not only showed himself only too eager to be caught in the snare that Corliss and Isabel so cleverly created and baited . . . he showed himself only too able to entice his huntress into the same, most treacherous, trap. . . .

(For a list of other Signet Regency Romances by Vanessa Gray, please turn page. . . .)

The
Orphan's
Disguise

Vanessa Gray

A SIGNET BOOK

NEW AMERICAN LIBRARY

NAL BOOKS ARE AVAILABLE AT QUANTITY DISCOUNTS
WHEN USED TO PROMOTE PRODUCTS OR SERVICES.
FOR INFORMATION PLEASE WRITE TO PREMIUM MARKETING DIVISION,
NEW AMERICAN LIBRARY, 1633 BROADWAY,
NEW YORK, NEW YORK 10019.

Copyright © 1986 by Vanessa Gray

Ⓢ

SIGNET, SIGNET CLASSIC, MENTOR, ONYX, PLUME, MERIDIAN
and NAL BOOKS are published by New American Library,
1633 Broadway, New York, New York 10019

First Printing, November, 1986

1 2 3 4 5 6 7 8 9

PRINTED IN THE UNITED STATES OF AMERICA

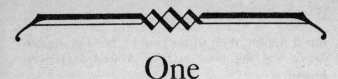

One

i

Corliss Hewett, aware of an unpleasant sinking sensation in the region of her stomach, paused in the doorway of the library at Hewett Manor. Accustomed to the shabbiness of its furnishings, a state that prevailed throughout the large house, she hardly noticed that the braid on her favorite chair had come loose and now hung down at a forlorn angle. The maid, Quinn, averse to unnecessary work, had not mentioned the damage, since she knew full well who would be required to do the needed repair.

Corliss's half-brother Ralph, who had summoned her in his usual peremptory manner, was alone in the room, engaged in reading intently a newly-arrived letter. From where Corliss stood, she could not make out the tiny script, except that she was quite sure the handwriting was not that of the lawyer in town who handled the Hewett affairs.

But if not his, then whose could it be? Correspondence was not thick on the ground at Hewett Manor.

Ralph was not one to encourage sociability. Not burdened with great intelligence, he found no satisfaction in conversation nor in reading.

He was, Corliss thought suddenly, excessively dull! Quickly, she suppressed such a disloyal thought. He was her half-brother, after all, and no matter how brusque he was with her, at bottom she believed he really loved her. However, that illusion, although she did not suspect it, was momentarily to be shattered.

Just now, he was as usual ignoring her. Perhaps if she crept away, he might forget he had sent for her. But she was made of sterner stuff, and she essayed a tentative, "You want to see me, Ralph?"

Sir Ralph Hewett looked up quickly, as though she had caught him in an indecency, and hastily thrust the letter into a desk drawer. Intrigued, she thought she had never until now recognized guilt written on his rather plain features.

"I had not expected you to respond so quickly, Corliss," he said, in the settled belief that mounting an offensive at once was the most satisfactory mode of conversation. Corliss was inured to this practice, having suffered it for too long from Ralph, and before him from their father, Sir Gervase. He continued, "Promptness is a virtue I had quite given up hope of instilling in you."

The ten years between their ages he regarded as giving him the right of a parent. In fact, he was her trustee, and until the next eighteen months had gone by, when she would arrive at the age of twenty-one, he was her guardian.

If Ralph had given up on teaching her promptness, he had succeeded, quite unwittingly, in instilling a certain wariness, such as an animal might learn. Corliss wisely did not protest his accusation. "Come in. Don't hover there in the doorway. Close the door behind you. No reason to confide our business to the servants."

As though we had, as we used to, a staff of fifteen, she thought, instead of the present meager number, parlor maid, cook, footman, and groom. Nonetheless, she closed the door behind her and sat near the mammoth desk that had belonged to Sir Gervase Hewett, only eleven months' dead.

What business could we have? she wondered. In her experience, the mention of business always meant some further sacrifice on her part. Her dear mare, Belle, had been sold shortly after their father had died. Then her own maid, Maggie, was dismissed, and when tottery old Burrows, the butler, had suffered a fatal stroke, his position was left empty.

"What do we need a butler for?" Ralph had argued. "We don't do any entertaining, not in this forsaken part of England, and God knows we can't cut a figure in London. No, we will do very well with only Samuel to answer the door. Not that we see anybody at the door above once a fortnight, when the vicar comes to call. Besides, all he wants is a glass of my father's port, and there's hardly enough left to keep *me* for a year. No, the vicar will soon tire of coming if there's nothing here to drink."

In this belief, Ralph was doing the vicar an injustice. It was true that the clerical visitations became less and less frequent, but the reason was not the fine cellar put down by Sir Gervase, or the dwindling amounts that were served, but the insulting, abrasive comments of Sir Ralph.

None of that was to the point this morning. Corliss, nervous, brushed back a dark curl that fell maddeningly over her forehead and shifted in her chair.

"What is it, Ralph? I collect it is something in that letter you put away in your desk?"

To her surprise, a faint flush appeared on her half-brother's sallow cheek. "No!" he said sharply. "That is, I have received a letter, one that concerns you nearly. I will read it to you."

He reached into a drawer and brought out a sheet of paper covered with large, spiky writing. Certainly not the same letter he had thrust so hastily out of sight, she was positive.

"It is from your cousin Elizabeth."

"Cousin Elizabeth!" Corliss exclaimed in tones of wonder. She had nearly forgotten that cousin Elizabeth existed. Ralph mistook her meaning.

"Yes, girl. Your cousin, your mother's cousin, of course. Lady Dacre," he said crossly. "From Yorkshire." Gratuitously, he added insult. "I suppose that expensive governess of yours taught you at least a smattering of geography? You do know where Yorkshire is?"

Used to such sarcasm—Ralph, not possessed of a scholarly bent, had dispensed with his own tutor by the simple means of making the man's life miserable, and then resented Corliss's governess and her superior education—she merely nodded.

"Lady Dacre has agreed to take you in, and I

think you must be excessively grateful to her for her kindness."

"Take me in?" Corliss was aroused. "Why on earth should she?"

"Because you cannot stay here. You know I only want what is best for you . . ." Whatever else he said went over Corliss's head, unheeded.

Take me in, like a waif from the workhouse? Abominable! She has never so much as acknowledged my existence, and why should she take me in when I am not in the least abandoned? What can he mean—I cannot stay here? I *live* here!

"Corliss! Sit down!" Ralph's voice came sharp as a bark. Corliss had not known she had leaped to her feet. "I had hoped we could settle this little affair without any acrimony. You must see that I am doing all this for your own good. You need to be with your mother's family now. Especially since there is so little money here. I cannot afford to keep you."

Suspicion roused in her, but, having little on which to grow, subsided. "But I don't understand. My trust fund from my mother—"

"Little enough. The interest is hardly sufficient to pay your board. You'll be better with Lady Dacre. She has excellent connections. Who knows," he finished with an elephantine gesture intended to be jocular, "she might even find you a husband!"

From what little Corliss had seen of the other gender, she had small desire to rush into matrimony. Her half-brother controlled her trust fund, and in truth, she had no idea of the terms of her mother's legacy to her—the funds had just seemed to come into Ralph's hands in some obscure way. Although her governess had given her excellent training in embroidery, in mending linen, in deportment, in playing the pianoforte, and even in singing melodic French tunes with an impeccable accent, Corliss occasionally became conscious of awesome gaps in her education, as now in her lack of understanding of her own financial affairs.

But it was too late to mend the deficiency.

"Then I have no money?"

"Lady Dacre has graciously consented to give you an allowance. She tells me that she has pleasant memories of your mother, and is willing to shelter you for her sake."

"What kind of allowance?"

Characteristically, upon being questioned Ralph gave rein to anger. "You will be fortunate indeed in simply having food to eat and a roof to sleep under. Lady Dacre has offered you a haven and you will be well advised to accept it with a cheerful mien, particularly since you have no choice in the matter."

Being adjured to put on a cheerful face inevitably resulted in Corliss's feeling obligated to pout. But since she was naturally a good-natured and hopeful young lady, her sullen expression lasted only a moment.

"Ralph, I don't understand—"

"You are not required to. I have noticed before— and you will recall that I have spoken to you about it more than once—you have a certain independence of spirit that bodes ill for your future. You must learn to curb your tongue, as well as your ridiculous sense of mischief. Your situation in life, as a female without wealth, is quite perilous enough without allowing yourself any unfortunate lapses that could not endear you to your cousin."

She caught one word of his scolding and pursued it. "What future will I have with Cousin Elizabeth?"

Or, she wondered for the first time, what future lay ready to hand, for that matter, here at Hewett Manor?

She had, from time to time, resented the fact that their father had not seen fit to provide separately for her welfare. His will all but ignored her very existence. Her income, even that from her small legacy from her mother, was dependent on the generosity of her half-brother. But after all, she too was a Hewett, and if the family, now reduced to just the two of them, was falling on hard times, then she must contribute all she could. She must not begrudge Ralph her infinitesimal—so she thought—trust fund income to help run the house.

The Hewett household, bereft of its formerly large staff, and the stables, nearly empty now, gave every indication of being run full tilt into the ground. It was impossible—speaking of the future as Ralph was—to imagine that ever a time would come when the fragile French wallpaper would be replaced, the lovely old damask draperies would be laid to rest after fifty years of arduous service in sunshine and—from failure to close windows promptly—in rain, or that new rugs would be laid in the vast salon.

If Corliss were honest with herself, those amenities were less exigent than the pleasantly remembered but bygone luxury of a small fire in the bedroom grate at bedtime and on frosty winter mornings.

"Why," wondered Corliss, "did not Cousin Elizabeth write to *me?*"

"Why should she?" countered Ralph. Besides, he thought, time enough for Corliss to discover Lady Dacre's character, as he had heard it described by his father—that of a crochety, gossipy, formidable woman who ran her servants to distraction. He had carefully not read the letter aloud to his stepsister. She would not, he thought with a grim smile, have been pleased to learn that Lady Dacre had written, "One cannot hope that she will exhibit any resemblance to her formidable grandmother, my Aunt Emma. I fear the younger generation is sadly lacking in manners, and even in starch. No stamina. I vow I outrun my entire staff. But I shall do my best to turn the child into a decent, presentable young lady." The implication was clear—her best would be quite sufficient to mold even the most recalcitrant baggage into an acceptable shape.

At the door Corliss, her thoughts tumbling out of control, turned and, for perhaps the first time in her life, challenged Ralph. "What if I refuse to go?"

Ralph stared at her, his pale blue eyes slightly protruding—like gooseberries, she thought irrelevantly—and sputtered. "No need to be impertinent, young lady."

"I simply wondered." She gazed at him, clearly expecting an answer.

He drew a deep breath, his cheeks flushed in anger. "You would be put on the stage by force," he said savagely, like a man pushed beyond endurance, "your trunk corded and strapped to the top, and you would see no alternative but to go to

Yorkshire, and be grateful that Lady Dacre has come to your rescue. I told you, Corliss, there is no room any longer for you here."

She left the library, and closed the door softly behind her. She longed to slam it with force sufficient to relieve her unwonted wrath.

No room for her anymore in the home she had known all her nineteen years? The house in which she had been born in that upstairs bedroom, the same room where her mother had died three years ago?

If that were true, if that were the way Ralph saw it, then there was no help for it—she must leave. She knew she could not abide living under the same roof with Ralph—not now, not after he had dismissed her rather like an unsatisfactory servant!

Later, her optimism would bubble as it always had to the surface. Later, in a few days, she might come to believe that perhaps Lady Dacre, Cousin Elizabeth as she must now call her, was not as heartless as she thought, even though she had never written to Corliss, not even to say she was sorry Corliss's mother had died.

But that would come later. Just now she paused in the entrance hall, aware that Samuel the footman was oddly blurred around the edges. Then she ran upstairs, blinded by furious tears, to the haven of her own room.

Earlier, Mrs. Potter, the cook, sensing that untoward events were about to transpire, had placed her eye to a judiciously narrow gap where by her hand the baize door to the kitchen wing stood ajar. Thus, she was in a prime position to view and correctly assess Corliss's state of mind.

The child had obviously received a great blow.

But what could be the nature of an upheaval that turned Corliss's cheeks to the color of ashes and caused tears to stream from her dark blue eyes?

When Corliss reached her bedroom, without knowing quite how she got there, she found Mrs. Potter, a trifle breathless from having hurried up the back stairs, waiting in the hall. Without thought, Corliss flung herself into that lady's comforting arms. Of her incoherent explanation, the cook discerned a few words that gave rise to substantial misgivings.

"Just come in and sit down, pet, and then you can tell me all about it. You've got mixed up somewhere, I don't doubt. Sending you away? What nonsense! He can't do that. This your *home*, child!"

The soothing words eventually had their effect on Corliss, even though her reaction was not precisely what Mrs. Potter had hoped. But at least Corliss grew quieter, and allowed her face to be washed in cool water, and her dress shaken out, and herself installed in one of the chairs near the fireplace. Her companion lowered herself cautiously in the other, hearing the mutinous squeal of wooden joints tested to their utmost under her substantial weight.

"Now, pet, tell me what's amiss. You've mistook something Mr. Ralph—Sir Ralph, that is—said, I'll be bound. Let's have it out, and you'll see there's naught to it."

Corliss was less agitated now. However, she had merely reached the calm of one who has traveled past civility into the far reaches of numbness. Mrs. Potter's heartening words scarcely touched her.

"Ralph is sending me away." Ignoring the sympathetic cluck of her comforter, she went on to explain in bald detail. "He's sending me to Mama's cousin Elizabeth—Lady Dacre, you know. I've never even *seen* her! Mama told me about her. Mama disliked her greatly, although I never knew why."

Mrs. Potter searched her memory, and found an echo of a long-ago quarrel between Sir Gervase and the second Lady Hewett. "If that damned cousin of yours has the effrontery to malign me—to tell you not to marry me—I tell *you* I won't have her in my house!" It was likely that at a later time Lady Hewett might have wished she had heeded her cousin's advice, but that was the way of the world, as Mrs. Potter knew well.

"Besides," Corliss sobbed anew, "he says I cost too much to keep!"

"That's nonsense, and he knows it! You don't cost anything to keep," the cook burst out. "Eat like a sparrow, you do. And goodness knows, he don't spend any money at all on your clothes, bar a new dress once a year or so from the seamstress in the village. And that's not a stylish gown, to be sure!"

"All I know is, he said I had to go. He's already arranged with Cousin Elizabeth to take me!"

Mrs. Potter patted Corliss's hand. Certainly, there was more to this than met the eye. She knew, however, that in the long run Corliss, not quite twenty, must do whatever Ralph ordered her to do. Young ladies must of necessity obey their guardians.

"I could run away," said Corliss in a small, speculative voice. "I could get a position as a—as a *kitchen* maid! Goodness knows, I've pared potatoes enough for you, dear Mrs. Potter."

Seeing her charge recovered sufficiently to be

left alone, Mrs. Potter exclaimed, "Speaking of
potatoes, that's done it! Time enough to be getting the master's meal." And, she added to herself, a good dose of rat poison for sauce, if I had
my way!

Patting the girl's hand again, Mrs. Potter rose to
leave. At the door, she said in a worried tone,
"Don't do anything daft, Corliss. You'd not last a
day as a kitchen maid."

"I promise. Besides, Ralph would come after
me. At least," she added dubiously, "I think he
would. Don't worry. I've not lost my senses."

Satisfied for the moment, Mrs. Potter returned
to her kitchen. She was not at all sure that Sir
Ralph Hewett, if he could send his stepsister away
in such a fashion, would in fact search for the girl
if she ran away. But Corliss had promised, so that
was all right. Whatever Sir Ralph had in his mind,
in Mrs. Potter's opinion, did not bear thinking on.
Nonetheless, experience informed her that she
would not in all probability like it.

In the meantime, Corliss, having cried herself
out, took a tentative peek into the future. She did
not like what she saw—a monstrous mansion, in
all likelihood, in the snow-covered dales of Yorkshire, and no escape possible if she could not
endure her cousin, for where could she go?

Corliss reminded herself, I promised to do nothing daft. Besides, if I ran away, I'd likely have to
change my name, and what name could I say?

Until the moment when she closed the library
door behind her, she had been aware that her
isolated life was rife with restrictions of an unpleasant nature. Now, faced with the prospect of

leaving Hewett Manor if not forever, at least for a measurable time, she began to cherish every item, no matter how neglected nor how much previously scorned.

However, one week was time enough for the idea of leaving Hewett Manor to become, if not eagerly anticipated, at least the lesser of two evils. For Ralph's temper deteriorated daily. He seemed to live beyond the far limits of his patience.

Mrs. Potter's cooking was, he told her more than once, invading her kitchen for the purpose, a disgrace. Why he himself could make shift to fix a duck so a man could digest it, even if she couldn't. And he, thank god, didn't call himself a cook!

He followed Quinn, peering suspiciously into the corners, as she performed her parlor maid duties until, as she proclaimed in the servants' hall, "I've a mind to shake that feather duster right in his snoopy face! He'd get a taste of feathers for certain. That duster has seen better days."

And Corliss was sent, more than once, sobbing to her room, following a devastating assessment of her disposition, her mental capabilities, and her probable future.

"Lady Dacre will have her hands full with you!" Ralph said, clearly happy at the prospect. It truly did not occur to her that there might be a reason for his irritable restlessness other than her own delinquency.

But Mrs. Potter came unwittingly near to the core of the force that drove him. "I swear it's sickening sometimes. There's no accounting for men," Mrs. Potter told the parlor maid. "Puts me in mind of Mr. Potter just before we got married. It was the worry did it." She paused, speculating.

"No, no, of course not. He'd be no catch for any lady, no money and all," she finished cryptically.

When the appointed day of departure arrived, Corliss set out, escorted only by Samuel, to take the stage at the stop nearest Hewett Manor, a small village just north of Bletchley. She was not surprised to realize that she was willing to exchange the devastating present for an unknown future. Ralph's constant verbal abuse had led her to be as anxious to escape from him as he clearly was to see her go.

She had been too cloistered to be proof against the enticing prospects of traveling away from Hewett Manor. Ralph was, Corliss knew, since her governess had carefully trained her in the niceties of social behavior, behaving with excessive miserliness, not to say scandalously. He had not bothered even to see her off. Nor had he furnished her with an abigail for company, perhaps already seeing her as a mere hireling herself in Lady Dacre's establishment and believing she might as well start as she was to go on.

Her possessions had been packed by Mrs. Potter, and pitifully small they were. Just before she closed the door for the last time, she took a long look around her room, conscious of a nagging sense of having mislaid something. Not her mother's miniature—that was safely stowed, swathed in her best linen nightshift, in her trunk. But—she had it! Her mother's brooch, a particularly fine opal surrounded by garnets—not of great intrinsic value, but her own. Her father, she remembered, had put the jewel away for safekeeping. However, it belonged to her and she meant to have it.

Ralph was not in the library. Although she did

not know it, he had purposely found errands that took him far in a direction opposite to that from which the stagecoach would appear, take Corliss aboard, and vanish out of his sight, and thus out of his thoughts.

Glancing around as guiltily as though she were about to rob a government vault, she went in. If she could recall correctly, Sir Gervase kept valuable items somewhere in the desk. She had watched him wrap her pin in a handkerchief and tuck it away. Would it still be there?

Which drawer, right or left?

Hastily, fearing to hear Ralph's footstep in the hall outside, she opened the center drawer first. An envelope caught her eye, and she recognized it as the one he had thrust hastily out of sight when he summoned her to hear her doom. With too much on her mind to be curious, she closed the drawer and continued her search.

The pin had been moved some time in the past, but only to the large lower drawer on the left side of the desk. There was a cash box, and a few loose sovereigns, as well as a small linen-wrapped object, in the drawer, but she had no interest save in her own property. Unwrapping the handkerchief only far enough to recognize that it was indeed her own pin, given her by her mother's own hand, she closed the drawer and hurried out into the hall.

"I'm ready!" she told the footman, far more brightly than she felt, and preceded Samuel, who bore her trunk on his shoulders, out of the house.

ii

When Ralph returned to the house, long after
Corliss had departed for the stage, he dropped
thankfully into the big chair in the library and
breathed a huge sigh of relief. He had cut it
rather too fine in his arrangements for Corliss,
but from this point on, all would go well.

He was due in Bath, at the house not far from
Henrietta Park, in only a sennight, and there was
a multitude of arrangements to be made before
then. Corliss's *congé* was only the first.

He leaned back in his chair. He was a thin,
rangy man, as his father had been. But unlike Sir
Gervase, Ralph wore a constant expression of ill
humor. Very few affairs went well for him, and
the only manner he knew to deal with misfortune
was a peevish one.

Now he contemplated the ceiling of his library,
only one of the many sources of anxiety which
wrinkled his unmemorable features. Where could
he find, for instance, a workman competent enough
to replace the plaster cupid lost from the corner
of the ceiling, where the damp had gotten in and
loosened the old Italianate plaster? How could his
fields, over which he had ridden only this morning, be brought up to prosperous production levels?

The only answer was to invest capital in the
dying estate. There had been no capital to use,
until Ralph had, by great good fortune, made a
rewarding discovery.

A rare smile touched his lips as he allowed his
mind to drift now with contentment over the

changes he planned to make in the near future. Fresh new cattle in the stables, new hangings in the public rooms, no doubt, and refurbishing of the chairs and sofas installed by his grandmother fifty years before and untouched except for periodic cleaning since then. New slates on the roof, perhaps. And after that, the Hewett fields . . .

Ralph had not suddenly fallen heir to the mines of Golconda, as his daydreams might have led one to suspect. In truth, he was planning—indeed had already offered and been accepted, via the missive in tiny script hastily hidden from Corliss—to marry Theresa Ludlow, a wealthy widow who was presently, with her young daughter, sojourning in Bath.

The widow of Bath's first husband, although in trade, had been a splendid catch for her, elevating her a few rungs on the social ladder. His fortune was large, and when he died, he left her his foundry, his ironmonger's trade, and their daughter Phyllida, a badly spoiled young woman of twelve.

Ralph suspected that his own charm for Theresa lay in his title, not his person. However, he was honest enough to admit that as a balance, his prospective bride's fortune held more appeal for him than her dumpy person.

Ralph and Theresa were united on at least one major point—the foundry and the trade were to be treated as though they did not exist. Surely Sir Ralph and Lady Hewett could arrange a better marriage for Phyllida if there were no odor of trade in the air.

Ralph did not look forward to the inevitable Season in London—but at the least four years must pass before the girl was ready to be offered on the Marriage Mart and he would be required to set foot in London, a city which, since a decade ago it had not welcomed him warmly, he abominated. And in those four years, much might be done to improve and augment the Hewett estates.

He had only a slight pang of regret at having to give Corliss her *congé*, so to speak. He had understood clearly that his intended bride intended to brook no interference in her new life. She had in fact refused to marry him until he could tell her that Corliss was no longer at home, a development he had anticipated before the fact in his most recent letter to Theresa. Although he did not understand women, he was in no doubt as to the inevitable discomfort to himself of having two mistresses of the household at the same time.

Besides, he comforted himself, Corliss was sure to have the best of the arrangement, living in the protective care of her cousin Elizabeth, and when the girl came of age, she would find her modest inheritance untouched, at least as to capital. That happy event he could not have promised without Theresa and her foundry. He was not the first of his quality to sacrifice breeding for money in a wife, nor would he be the last.

In the meantime, he would be a married man in seven days. He sighed again with contentment. Corliss was on her way north to Lady Dacre. His own future was relatively unclouded.

What could go wrong? Nothing!

iii

Nothing, thought Lady Dacre, could go wrong.

After many years of uncomfortable estrangement from her young cousin Fanny, of whom she had been excessively fond, at last dear Fanny's daughter Corliss would soon be on her way north to Dacre Hall, near Helmsley in Yorkshire, to provide comfort and company to her in her declining years.

Lady Dacre, a woman of middle years, was a comfortable woman, padded like a chair, with a forgiving nature. Her hair, which her maid Towne was dressing at the moment, was a cloud of light brown, touched with gray. Her eyes were the color of lapis lazuli, as dark a blue as Corliss's—a family trait.

Lady Dacre gave to her servants and friends an impression of softness, but underneath, buried beneath years of easy living, she was still capable if need be of decisive, even swift, action.

Ralph would have been surprised to learn that his unfavorable opinion of Lady Dacre's character was not entirely accurate, bequeathed to him, as it were, from his father, who had reason enough to dislike the lady. The truth was that Lady Dacre was pleased to contemplate the healing of the long-standing rift between herself and dear Fanny's family. Family disagreements were always so unpleasant—one constantly had to think what not to say, and to whom.

Not that this particular rift was of the sort that

shattered the family and grew to proportions that scandalized—and excited—civilized society. Oh, no!

And Lady Dacre could not, she told herself stoutly, be blamed in the least for the trouble between herself and dear Fanny. She had merely expressed her opinion—rather vigorously, as it happened—on the inadvisability of Fanny's marriage to that nonentity Sir Gervase Hewett. A man of limited intelligence and a distressing dislike of society, possessed of a great hulking motherless son—the match, so said Lady Dacre, was totally ineligible.

And now, some twenty years later, that same hulking son was sending dear Fanny's daughter to Lady Dacre.

"Mark my words, my lady," said Lady Dacre's faithful, jealous personal maid, Towne, "she'll be nothing but trouble to you. Young people these days—well, it wouldn't surprise me but what she'll want parties and horses and clothes and all kinds of carrying-on."

"Now, Towne," said her mistress comfortably, "that surely will not concern you? I know you have little patience with young people, as I fear I do myself. But it does occur to me that perhaps my dislike is only because I am acquainted with so few of them. That young ruffian, the squire's son, for instance. I heard that at the last Assembly ball he fell from his horse three times before he got home. A gentleman holds his drink better than that, I assure you!"

"Her maid will want a room to herself, I suppose," resumed Towne as though Lady Dacre had not spoken. "Flint will put her in the northwest room next to the chimney. A very comfortable room. Where it's warm!" she finished in a tolerable imitation of Flint at his most pompous. "She'll be pretty, likely, and Flint—" She broke off, remembering her mistress's dislike of gossip.

Presently Lady Dacre, following her own thoughts, resumed. "And I rather fancy I will know how to deal. I have not opened the house in town for these fifteen years. It might be pleasant to visit London again."

Towne concentrated on Lady Dacre's hairdress, trying to emulate an arrangement she had seen in the *Ladies' Monthly Museum*, designated as Breath of Spring. When she spoke again, she approached the subject from another direction. She knew her mistress thoroughly, and cunningly probed a well-known weakness.

"We'll have to stay home then," she said in a brisk manner. "Too bad, my lady, that you must miss your visit to Scarborough, even though the waters would do you good." She sighed heavily. "Shall I tell Flint to change your arrangements?"

Lady Dacre bristled. Her semiannual journey to take the waters at Scarborough, to hear the notable visiting lecturers on subjects she did not understand but which sounded grand and important, and to partake of the other entertainment devised for the invalid and for the merely bored, like Lady Dacre herself . . . No, it would not be at all necessary sacrifice her few pleasures. Fanny's girl might come when she wished, and Flint would make her comfortable. That foolish half-brother of hers had not mentioned a date. At any rate, she herself would likely be back from Scarborough before Corliss arrived.

Towne repeated her question. "Shall I tell—?"

Lady Dacre interrupted. "Tell him nothing, Towne. We will travel as planned.

Towne, satisfied by her victory, hid her smile. She said only, "I've laid out the dark blue for this morning, my lady." If only she didn't take it into her head to go to that dirty, nasty London, thought Towne darkly. I should hope, she unconsciously echoed her mistress, I shall know how to deal with that folly!

iv

London was indeed dirty, thought Margaret Garnett dispiritedly, but it was that man Mr. Ackley who was nasty.

"I vow I have such a headache!" she sighed. "I wish I could pass it to Mr. Ackley. After all, he gave it to me."

"Poor Mama," sympathized her daughter Isabel, who was her sole companion in London. She put her hand under her mother's elbow and looked into her face. "Mama, you look truly ill! Let's abandon our plans for this afternoon so you may go back to the hotel and rest. I do not need to see Lord Elgin's marbles on this occasion. I am sure they will not crumble away."

"We may never have another visit to London," said Mrs. Garnett drily. Nonetheless, she turned back, at Isabel's gentle urging, toward Pulteney's.

The two—mother and daughter—made a strange pair. Mrs. Garnett was soberly dressed in half-mourning, as befitted a widow of six months. Her young companion, a sweet-faced young lady of sixteen, of obviously excellent breeding, was incongruously dressed in a plain round gown of a color and fabric more often associated with women of the servant class.

There was nothing of subservience in the girl's manner, however, save for an infrequent moment when it seemed as though she must have remembered the impression she meant to give. A spectator might be irresistibly reminded of an inexperienced *Twelfth Night* Viola, striving to appear as something she was not.

Since papa had died, leaving all those debts that must paid, and which took all their funds, the Garnetts were living on the small income from Mrs. Garnett's settlement, which the creditors had been unable to attach.

Isabel was the oldest of five children, and she knew there were unpleasant facts to be faced now that Mr. Ackley had closed the last door in their faces. One was that there would, barring an unexpected miracle, be no Season for her in London nor likely a suitable marriage, nor would her next brother, Geoffrey, have the opportunity to get a Cambridge education, as befitted his position.

And the fate of the three younger children, Sophia, Augustus, and young Jerome, still in leading strings, was now so uncertain as not to be thought of.

"That dreadful Mr. Ackley," said Mrs. Garnett later, lying on her bed with a cold, wet cloth over her eyes. "He would not even agree to tell Douglas Renfrew of my visit, to say nothing of recommending that your grandfather's unentailed income come to us now instead of waiting until Douglas marries. That infamous will! Isabel, do you mind so very much pretending to be my maid?"

"Certainly not," said Isabel stoutly. "It's really great fun. No different really from the charades we like to play. Besides, I know we cannot afford the extra fare for a servant, and surely Nellie would be of no use to you here in town, even if you could get her on a stagecoach. She will scarcely get into a farm cart to go to the village. I've never seen such a flighty, stupid girl!"

"You must not blame Nellie. Some people are terribly afraid of what they don't understand, or don't see clearly. As I must confess I am myself, since your father died. I don't see how we are to manage at all! If only your great-grandfather had not married that dreadful woman!"

Isabel knew the story well enough. Her grandfather had fallen desperately in love with youth and springtime and new beginnings, as an old man is prone to do. Unfortunately, his illusions took the shape of a greedy and excessively vulgar actress, who inevitably left him, taking all the money and jewels she could lay hands on.

His reaction had been swift, if not entirely predictable. Most of his substantial wealth was entailed upon his grandson, Douglas Renfrew, but that which was not he willed to Douglas on condition that he not marry. The merest indication of an intention to wed would whisk that money away and bestow it on George Garnett, the only grandson living at the time.

"I had not realized how much I had counted on Colonel Renfrew's being amenable to the reversion of that income," Mrs. Garnett continued. "I can't think why Mr. Ackley thinks Douglas needs it. He has all the entailed estates, after all, and I would count that as the wealth of the Indies!"

"That wretched will of Grandfather's," said Isabel with scorn. "Just because he was no judge of character, especially women, we must all suffer."

Mrs. Garnett tore the cold cloth from her eyes and raised herself to lean on one elbow. Fixing her daughter with a gaze filled with disappointment and helplessness, she said, "If only Colonel Renfrew would marry! That would solve our problem. But how on earth is he to find a wife on the Peninsula? In wartime?"

"Maybe he will come back with a gorgeous Spanish noblewoman with a mantilla and long ruffled shawls. Would that count as a marriage?"

"Even a betrothal, so long as it is public, will suit our needs. But I really doubt," said Mrs. Garnett drily, "that Spanish duchesses would be plentiful in the midst of battle."

"Then," said Isabel extravagantly, with the sole purpose of cheering her mother, "we shall simply have to trick him."

"Isabel!" said Mrs. Garnett, startled. "You are only joking, of course. I would write to him, regardless of Mr. Ackley, but I haven't the slightest notion of how to reach him." She sank back on the pillow and lapsed into thoughtful silence.

At length, regretfully, she said, "No, no. Douglas Renfrew is beyond our reach, even by trickery, which of course I could not condone."

V

Colonel Douglas Renfrew, contemplating with mixed feelings the end of his long stint with His Majesty's forces in the Peninsular War, sat, as befitted an invalid, on a campstool beside his luggage on the waterfront at Vigo. The last truly malignant attack of ague had weakened him to the point where the duke himself had sent him on his way back to England.

"You've earned a leave in England," said the duke. "How long since you've been home?"

"Five years," said the colonel. They were sitting on camp chairs in the duke's command tent. The flaps were open to catch what breeze might find its way up the hill.

"Not even seen your new estates?"

Renfrew shook his head, and wished he hadn't as a malarial pain shot through behind his eyeballs. "All I know is my grandfather's estate was entailed on my father. Since he's been dead for a few years, the lot comes to me." He laughed ruefully. "The old man lived as long as Methuselah— seventy his past birthday! I thought Napoleon's sharpshooters would do for me long before this, and someone else could worry about the estates."

His gaze lingered now on the scene outside the duke's tent. He saw the orderly chaos of a military camp, set against a background of brown hills and bright blue sky. He would miss all this, but perhaps not as much as he would if his health were perfect. As it was, the sunlight made his eyes ache and the oppressive heat drained his strength.

The duke, looking with compassion at his friend, saw features which had become as familiar to him as a brother's over the years of army service. A strong face, though not handsome, thought the duke, reflecting a character resolute and sometimes bold to the point of rashness. He would miss Renfrew, but the French were nearly finished in Spain and the colonel could be spared. In truth, the colonel was of no present use in his state.

At least the duke had seen to it that Colonel Renfrew did not travel alone. Now, on the wharf, Colonel Renfrew looked up when his aide, Captain Wheeler, came back to his side, accompanied by ruffianly looking porters in the charge of the colonel's batman, who had been with him since he landed in Spain, too long ago to think about now.

Charles Wheeler eyed his colonel with misgivings. "I've seen you looking better. Never mind, we'll be aboard in a few minutes," he reassured him, "and find your cabin."

"I'm not an invalid!" said Colonel Renfrew mendaciously. "All I need is a shady spot to sit. That doctor said the sea voyage would work miracles." Leaning rather heavily on his aide's arm, he began his slow progress toward the small boat that would take him to the schooner riding at anchor in the famous harbor. "I'll accept any miracles that come my way," he finished with a wry smile.

A few days later he was ready to admit that the doctor had known what he was talking about. "You look yourself again," said the captain. "By the time we get to England, we'll be ready to dance away the night at Almack's."

"I doubt I'll ever be ready for that," said the colonel. "But after a fortnight at Bath, I'll be ready to deal with Ackley. I'm not at all happy with the reports he's been sending me."

"You think he's embezzled the lot?"

"He was my grandfather's man, and my father's during his lifetime, so I doubt Ackley would steal. But his reports are too brief. Surely there is more going on with the farms and all than he tells me."

He glanced at his friend, leaning against the rail, watching the water creaming along the ship's side. "What are you thinking about, Charles?"

"About how good it will be to see a woman again, any woman with blue eyes, and golden ringlets, and a fair skin the texture of rose petals—I've had my fill of brunette beauties!"

"Take care you don't get leg-shackled before you know it."

"Ah, but Douglas, I only pursue young girls of the lower ranks of society. No question of getting caught by the parson's mouse trap, you know." He grinned, in anticipation of delights to come. "I don't harm them, you know. There's not a female in England who has come to any harm through me."

"In England," repeated the colonel.

"I swear it. But as to this hellhole we're just out of, well, a hot sun does its work, you know."

With a laugh, Douglas commented, "You'll cool off well enough in Bath. We may count ourselves well off if it doesn't rain the entire two weeks we are there. Expect a dull time, Charles!"

After the excitement and danger of unceasing war, Charles thought, he should be glad of a quiet time. But his lips twisted wryly as he responded.

"Enchanting," he said.

Two

i

The stagecoach was still out of sight around a bend in the road when Corliss reached the village, but the commanding note of the horn warned all would-be passengers to be ready.

Samuel, his duty discharged, set her trunk on the ground, not gently, touched his forehead to her, and departed. Her last link with home, she thought, and he could not wait to be gone.

At last the six horses, blowing and shaking their heads, appeared, and the yellow coach itself thundered on their heels. She felt an odd *frisson* at her first sight of the very vehicle which was to bear her away from all she loved into a misty unknown.

The coach drew up in a vast and billowing cloud of dust. The outside riders dropped to the ground, coughing as they sought clearer air. The doors opened, and Corliss stood looking up into the

vehicle, seeing nothing but a mishmash of skirts
and trouser legs, a basket probably containing provisions for a long journey, and a lady's bandbox.
Corliss willed herself not to allow tears to brim in
her eyes. There was no room for her—anywhere!
The thought came perilously near to overwhelming her. Then she blinked hard and was herself
again.

One of the trouser legs moved, and then a matching one, and their owner winkled himself out of
the tight pack of bodies wedged in the enforced
intimacy of the coach.

"Here, now, miss," he said with an air, "there's
room for all in the coach. Take my word for it,
miss, they sold you a ticket, you've got a place."

Her relieved smile was unconsciously radiant.
"But you must not give me your seat!"

"Whyever not?" he said. "Confidentially"—he
leaned closer— "air's pretty fusty in there. I'll be
glad to ride up top, where I can breathe."

Then, taking in the deep blue eyes and the
brown ringlets teased by a wayward breeze, he
glanced around him and noted she was the only
boarding passenger. "How far are you traveling,
young miss?" She was aware of an odd note of
familiarity that had crept into his voice. He must
believe her to be a servant, traveling alone as she
was. A small resentment of Ralph's parsimony
flared. However, her long-ago governess had taught
her well. She moved not an inch, but the man
recognized that she had suddenly put him in his
place.

"I thank you for your courtesy, sir," she said,
and at the tone of her voice he reddened. "Is

that my trunk being corded at the boot? I see it is."

Hands reached out from the interior of the coach and pulled her up. From the corner of her eye she caught sight of a pair of trousered legs twinkling out of sight as the recent inside passenger swung himself up to the roof of the coach, and the vehicle jerked forward abruptly as the horses bent into the harness. Corliss lost her balance and fell against the next passenger, and apologized.

She was aboard the coach at last, her arms pinned to her sides by the bodies of the passengers on either side of her like a trussed fowl. She wondered why all the others had taken passage, where they had come from, where they were going.

As for herself, she knew well where she had come from, and she was on her way to a future of which she entertained the liveliest dread.

ii

She had certainly started out, she thought after she had caught her breath and been reassured that her heart was slowing down, in the most embarrassing way possible, recalling the small incident with the forward young man. Now that she had had time to think, it came clearly to her that, dressed as she was in a simple round gown, obviously not new, with an unfashionable shawl around her shoulders, she must appear to everyone at first as a servant.

Perhaps not a kitchen maid, as she had pro-
posed in jest to Mrs. Potter, who had rightly scoffed
at the notion, for her hands were not red and
chapped, but certainly she must appear to belong
to one of the lower orders. No wonder the young
gallant had mistaken her quality.

Besides, to be proper, she should have been
accompanied by her own maid. The trouble was
that there was no one at Hewett Manor who could
be spared. Indeed, if Ralph were so scraped for
money, he might not have been able even to afford the coach fare for a maid.

Besides—although Corliss did not think this
through very clearly—certainly Lady Dacre's plans
for her must not include such state as having her
own maid, or she would have sent funds for the
maid's fare.

The possibility that occurred to her was unwel-
come but very persistent. There was no doubt of it
in her mind—Lady Dacre was expecting to get a
maid of her own at very little cost! She made a
small *moue*.

Her unconscious grimace was not unseen. A
voice spoke at her right, saying, "He was brash
indeed, wasn't he?" The voice was cultured, upper
class, and amused. "You did that very well. No
need though to give him another thought."

Corliss turned gratefully. "How kind you are!
But in truth . . ."

In truth, what? The man was justified from my
appearance? Could she say, I've been sent away
from my own home to work as a servant for a
woman I do not know? How gothic! Her neighbor
waited for her to continue, but Corliss, feeling

suddenly very much alone, could not speak over the lump in her throat.

She managed to smile, shyly, and the passengers rode on in silence, if one did not count the rumbling of the great wheels, the hard rhythm of the horses' hooves, the crack of a whip at intervals. As a diversion, she looked around her at the other passengers.

The woman who had first spoken to her, in that amused fashion that invited Corliss to share in a merry view of the world, was moderately well dressed—although Corliss noted a tiny darn in the finger of one glove. She was of mature years, but the years had for the most part treated her kindly. There were wrinkles which looked new at the corners of her fine gray eyes, and a certain nervousness that displayed itself in her moving fingers.

On the other side of this woman was another, who could have been the same age. Corliss, with more experience, might have noticed the arid, taut look around her eyes, and an uncompromising tightness in the thin lips. Opposite that woman, and connected in some way with her, sat a man of indeterminate age with a clerical collar and brooding eyes.

And directly opposite Corliss was a very pretty girl, younger even than Corliss, she thought. Her ringlets, peeping out from a plain bonnet, were golden, and her skin was smooth as rose petals. She sat primly with downcast eyes, the very picture of a lady's maid, and Corliss realized with dismay that her own appearance duplicated the other's in so many details, it was of little use to remember that she herself was a young lady of quality, if not means. She was dressed like a maid, she appeared to be a maid—and if Lady Dacre's plans went through, she would doubtless *be* a maid.

While a part of her had, this past week, begun to explore a world she did not know, the world beyond the walls of Hewett Manor, the part that stayed uppermost in her mind at this moment was, that travel had some drawbacks.

Still, optimistic as was her habit, she had not reached the end of her journey, and there was much to enjoy at present. She looked up to see the maid opposite watching her. An elfin grin touched the girl's lips, and Corliss was drawn to respond. The maid glanced at the cleric's wife—no, she must be his sister—and by some alchemy conveyed to Corliss her idea that the cleric's sister was one poor stick and probably much to be pitied!

Almost as though in answer to the maid's unspoken opinion, the vicar's sister broke the silence inside the coach. "All sitting here," she began as though finishing a sentence already begun in her mind, "in indecent proximity, it is a disgrace. Pray put up that curtain, Brother, to keep at least some of the dust out."

It was clear to Corliss that the vicar's black-clad sister resented her journey on the stagecoach. No doubt from her first view of the coach, probably in Swann's yard, she considered this journey another step on the downgrading of her way of life. Her voice was peevish, and she punctuated her words with an annoying and genteel sniff.

"I shall miss London," she said flatly, changing the subject and addressing the older lady. "There is so much going on, you know, with parties and teas, and although with my brother being a man of the cloth I did not wish to make myself conspicuous in society, yet—" her lips twitched with satisfaction— "yet, one has one's friends to keep one *au courant*."

Clearly wishing to be questioned as to the latest rumors running amok in London, she paused. When no one inquired, she set to remedy the lack. "That dreadful Frenchman—although I believe he is not French, but no matter—he has been soundly defeated, I hear, and we will have the dear duke home once again with us. I am sure he will have some quite dreadful stories to tell about his experiences with the natives—"

"The natives," said her brother, roused to speech, "are perfectly respectable Spanish people."

"Foreigners, Joshua, you cannot get away from that. And of course, you must agree that the war is nearly over. Surely Wellington would not send home his regiments without reason."

Corliss saw the faintest of clouds pass over the face of the older woman. Was her distress, well dissembled though it was, due to recollection of a soldier in her own family? Corliss, entertaining herself by speculating, decided that at least the soldier, if he existed, must not have been killed for the frown did not seem deep enough for grief.

Corliss had taken a fancy to the lady. She was quite pretty, and very kind in her response to the other woman's inane chatter. Now she was asking about the poor mad king, and names which were unknown to Corliss but were probably famous emerged in the idle conversation. It was as though a door opened before Corliss's very eyes. A world apart existed in London. People lived and died and met each other for dinner and entertained at tea, and all shopped at the same fashionable emporiums and tripped along the walks and allowed the crossing sweepers to clear a path for them through unspeakable gutter debris, and—

And suddenly Corliss became aware, as though by a sudden illumination, that the other world she was now hearing about, the world of London society, could have been her own world were circumstances different. Had her mother lived, had there been money, had Ralph stirred himself . . .

But there was no money, and therefore it made little difference whether Ralph stirred himself or not.

Thoughts came rushing to her, and her companions in the packed coach faded into nothing. She had been expected once to take her place in that world—so much she knew; how else would one explain her careful training by the governess—until Ralph dismissed her. She knew full well that she was gently born, that she came of good if not famous family—

The stagecoach crossed over a humpback bridge, climbed a steep curving hill, and shuddered to a stop. They could hear shouts and the pounding of running feet.

"Highwaymen!" shrilled the vicar's sister in a strangled voice. "I told you," she added viciously to her brother, "that I should never like the country. From this moment forward I shall never lay my head on my pillow without expecting it to be off my shoulders by morning."

Corliss blinked at this somewhat convoluted prophecy, but the reason for the sudden stop became evident before she could give thought to it.

One of the passengers from the roof dropped lightly to the ground and looked in the window. "Nothing to worry about, ladies. It's only a steep hill down to the next valley, and they must skid up." Grinning at the bewildered expression on Corliss's mobile features, he added, "No brakes, don't you see."

The process was simple, even though the words they used to describe it were as in a foreign tongue. The coach had no mechanical brakes, and rather than plummet downhill at such a great rate as to overrun the horses, even if the coach did not smash itself by overturning on the steep slope, the guard must attach a dragshoe, made of iron, under the near hind wheel.

"Sometimes, I am told," said the vicar's sister, looking more than ever like a bird of prey—or rather a scavenger, thought Corliss, brooding over the prospect of an early dinner—"the skids get so hot, going down a steep decline, that they damage the wheel. And on the next curve, a dreadful catastrophe. Joshua— "

The vicar had been goaded sufficiently. In a rather pathetic gesture of defiance, he said, "Amelia, I did not ask you to come with me."

The expression on his sister's face was mixed. Indignation, embarrassment, and an acute desire for revenge fought for dominance on Amelia's sharp features. Corliss, looking anywhere but at the clerical pair, caught the eye of the demure miss sitting across from her. She was obviously an abigail, in attendance on the older lady, but there

was something indefinably different about her.
Corliss found it difficult to think of her in the
same way as she had her own Maggie.

Especially difficult, she thought, as the maid
gave her the merest hint of an merry wink.

iii

It was clear, thought Corliss, that she had a lot
to learn between now and her arrival at Cousin
Elizabeth's. All maids were not like Maggie, good-
hearted, clumsy, uneducated, and prone to rash
behavior.

Rash behavior? Corliss herself was wound up as
tightly as a drumhead from the enormous change
that had taken place in her life, the stimulus of
the stagecoach, the headlong journey into an unknown future. Now to her great dismay she found
herself trembling on the verge of unseemly laughter. She recognized the same impulse in the maid
opposite, and it was too much.

Corliss muffled a sort of giggling snort, and
clasped her fingers tightly enough to hurt. She
began to entertain a vague doubt about the girl
across from her—surely this was behavior unbe-
coming a maidservant?

She stole a sidelong glance at the girl's mistress,
and surprised a powerful frown on that lady's
brow. Instead of quelling the maid, it only set her
off again. Of course the lady could not chastise
her in public, but Corliss suddenly understood
that the girl's punishment, whatever it might be,

would not be too harsh, for there was the slightest trembling at the corner of the lady's gently curving lips.

Hastily, Corliss looked out the window, trying to regain her own control. This was quite the oddest day she had ever spent, huddled together with a group of motley strangers, hurtling through the countryside on her way to—who knew what?

Her impulse to laugh had quite disappeared. Indeed, she thought, she would be well out of this if she managed not to break down in sobs. Homesickness, that's what it was. She would not admit to fear of the unknown, or regret at the lost glitter of the vicar's sister's world, which she would never know.

The coach had been descending the long hill, obedient to the barrier provided by the dragshoe. Now they seemed to have arrived in the valley.

The older lady and Corliss's near-accomplice in disgrace began to gather themselves together, with the clear intention of leaving the stage at the next stop.

Suddenly, Corliss dreaded being left with the vicar and his sister, and most likely the roof passengers would descend and sit next to her, and— But perhaps someone new would get on, she thought, and her spirits rose.

None of the eventualities she envisioned did in fact come about—at least, none that she had worried about.

iv

Later, she thought it could only have been the
emotional strain under which she labored that led
to the disaster. Trying to keep from crying with
simple desperate homesickness for a home that
was no longer hers, or with simple apprehension
of the frightening unknown future that lay ahead,
would have been hard enough. But add to that
the need to quell the waves of laughter, just a bit
hysterical, if truth be told, and she had—she realized later—all the ingredients to stir up trouble.

One of the young men from the roof stood at
the open door of the coach, offering his hand to
help her to the ground. The older lady and her
maid stood a few steps away, supervising the rec-
lamation of their luggage from the boot. The vicar
and his sister, no longer speaking, sat stiffly still in
their seats.

Lifting her skirt a trifle so that she could reach
the step, Corliss reached for the man's hand. The
dust raised by the carriage wheels still swirled
lazily, reaching her eyes. She blinked in vain, and
her eyes teared and blurred. She missed her foot-
ing and tumbled forward.

And the next thing she knew she lay on the
ground, her dignity totally shattered. Her bonnet
slid to one side of her head, her cheek felt the
pain of sharp impact on the abrasive gravel. She
was mortified. She longed for the ground to open
up and swallow her in her entirety.

Her luck, at least in that regard, was not in.

Instead of being swallowed up, ignored, she was the center of an exclaiming throng.

"She didn't have my hand," said the would-be gallant. "She didn't take my hand. She reached, but she didn't take my hand. She should have—"

"Stow it!" shouted a commanding voice.

"How did it happen?"

"Her own fault, that's what it is." This was the coachman. "Can't blame the company for that. She just—"

A voice much closer, and much more gentle, spoke. "Pray go away, all of you. Just give the child a chance to breathe. Oh, do stand back!" Corliss moved convulsively. "Not you, my child. I am persuaded that the slightest movement must be agony for you. Just lie back. You must let us decide what is best for you."

Gladly, thought Corliss. Her ankle seemed one mass of pain, and she felt with some alarm that her shoe had suddenly shrunk.

"Where does it hurt?"

That was a sensible question, Corliss thought, in her vagueness. How had it happened? She hadn't the slightest idea. But where it hurt—now *that* she knew.

"My—my ankle," she mumbled, struggling to sit up. Her skirts were awry—how embarrassing! She felt that even her bones were blushing.

"Will one of you please help me? She cannot be heavy," said the soft voice.

Strong arms came under Corliss and lifted her. She cried out with the pain of movement. If only she could lie down, perfectly still, perhaps the pain would go away. At bottom, she knew she had sustained a bad injury. But people were helping and she must not distress them by screaming, and the march to the inn was accomplished quickly.

They put her down on a small settee in a private sitting room. She leaned back and closed her eyes. "Just let me sit a moment," she said. "I'll be fine."

Waves of pain swept through her, but even worse was the sense of having sustained a great shock, as though she had been struck with a club. The ground, no doubt. She began to shake.

"Here, Isabel, put my cloak over her."

When at last she opened her eyes, she saw that she was in the midst of a great company. The older lady from the stagecoach—hers was the gentle, authoritative voice—her maidservant, and even the vicar and his sister all watched her intently.

A man she had not seen before—most likely one of the roof passengers—knelt in front of her. He looked up at her, his square face sunburned like a countryman's, and said, "By your leave, missy, I think I'd best have a look."

His rough-skinned hands busied themselves with her ankle, thrusting her petticoat up out of the way. The farmer clucked audibly. "A great swelling, missy. Let's see what's amiss. That hurt?" he asked her, his touch gentle on her, "Or this?"

Her answers apparently were satisfactory, for her skirts were pulled down, her feet were swung up to the settee. "Merely a sprain," he said.

"Are you a doctor, sir?"

"No, but you don't need a quack for this. I know about horses, don't you know, and one joint is much like another. You'll need to keep off that ankle for a bit, let the swelling go down."

"How about a bran fomentation?" said another male voice. "That's what I use on my cattle."

The soft voice of the older lady said, "The child is not a colt, you know."

"Couldn't hurt," said the first man, "to try."

The coachman bustled in, anxious not on Corliss's account, but mindful of his schedule and his employers.

"No bones broken, I hear? Not my fault, you all saw that. She missed the step."

The farmer turned on him. "You said all that before. Now button it."

Suddenly Corliss, assured that no bones were broken, remembered her situation. Struggling to sit up, she cried out, "No, no. I cannot. I must be on the stage. Don't let it go without me!"

"Best hurry then, miss. I've got my schedule to keep," admonished the coachman.

"Very well," she said, "I'll be there," and swung her feet to the floor. Pain shot up her leg, and she fell back onto the settee. "In a minute," she gasped. For the first time she ventured to look for herself at the offending ankle. *Swollen*, was the first word that came to her. The second was, the skin will burst!"

"You see, my child," said her new friend, the older lady, "you really cannot travel on."

"But—I must! What else can I do!"

Her eyes fell on the landlord, standing behind the others. She was not impressed. Shabbiness she was accustomed to, mending and make-do were second nature to her, but dirt she was not prepared for.

Besides the scruffy appearance of the man himself, his inn showed up to no better advantage. There was dirt that dated, she thought, from the previous century, ingrained in the window sill and the tables. The floor could not been scrubbed within living memory. She pulled her skirt to her, as though to minimize its contact with whatever crawled in the grimy cushions. The movement made her ankle twinge sharply, and she winced.

Through the sitting-room door she could see the public bar. A shelf stood behind it, containing pewter tankards either tarnished or so thick with dust that the material they were made of was indistinguishable.

"Come on, miss, make up your mind," said the coachman impatiently.

Corliss gathered her strength. To stand up was almost beyond her, but to take a step, knowing the pain would return with a vengeance, was almost more than she could face. She reached out for strong hands, which obligingly allowed her to pull herself gingerly to her feet.

So far, so good. The pain was not minimal, but not overwhelming, until she took a step on the injured ankle. A dreadful moan was wrung from her. She took another step before she collapsed into the arms of the man who had so expertly probed her ankle.

"What can I ever do?" she repeated almost to herself.

"Stay here," suggested the farmer. "Landlord will give you a room."

"Not without some gelt, I won't," said the landlord.

Whether it was the mention of money or not,

the crowd around her suddenly thinned until she was left with the older lady, and her maid. The coachman paused at the door. "If you can't make it any farther then that, you can't ride in my coach."

"I could be carried!" Corliss suggested, looking hopefully at him.

"Won't have it! Don't want any trouble. You others—better climb in fast. Coach is leaving right now."

Corliss, determined but ill-advised, essayed another step toward the door, with the idea of getting as far as the coach and letting what came next take care of itself. The doorway blurred before her. Darkness swirled in on her. She heard the rumble of coach wheels as though from a great distance, and knew no more.

Three

i

She was away from herself only briefly, but in that short space of time much had been decided. The coach had gone, taking most of the passengers with it. At the door of the parlor, looking out at something or someone, stood the older lady.

"Oh!" exclaimed Corliss faintly. "You did not miss the coach on my account, did you? You should not have done so!"

The woman turned quickly. Her smile could not have been sweeter, thought Corliss, tears starting, if she had been Corliss's own mother.

"Of course not. We live nearby. Are you feeling better now? Do you feel you could hobble a few steps if we help you?" Taking note of the open bewilderment on Corliss's features, she hastened to add, "I am Mrs. Garnett. My son Geoffrey has come to meet us with the carriage. He'll be here in a minute."

Indeed, Corliss could hear approaching voices, raised in altercation. The masculine voice sounded aggrieved.

"All these trunks, Bel? I vow you had not so many when you left."

"Of course not, stupid." Corliss recognized the voice of the girl she had thought at first was a maidservant. But no servant ever called the young man of the house stupid. "I told you, we have a guest. That trunk is hers, and her bandbox is around someplace. Oh, there it is!"

"Point is," said the young man, who must be Geoffrey, "did you do any good in London? Old Chalmers was around again!"

"Not so loud. You can't want everyone to hear about—"

The voices were lowered and Corliss could hear no more. Absently, she moved her foot, and regretted it excessively. She gasped.

"Poor child!" soothed Mr. Garnett. "You'll feel better soon."

"I don't understand," fretted Corliss. "What is to happen next?"

"You're coming home with us."

"Oh, no, I cannot! It would be too bad of me to impose on strangers'

"I will not be at all comfortable thinking of you here at the inn. Alone. Pray don't object. After all, the landlord is a stranger to you also."

As is the whole world now, Corliss suddenly remembered. She had not thought of her situation quite in that light before.

And certainly these strangers were more comforting than her brother had ever been!

"But—"

She was told to hush. "You'll stay with us," said Mrs. Garnett, "and I do not wish to hear any argument."

Geoffrey came in and was introduced. "We can get you to the carriage, miss," he told her. "You must not be heavier than Isabel. I can carry you."

Corliss was beyond argument. The pain in her swollen ankle was worse, throbbing insistently, and she knew she was helpless. With some relief, she realized she must be content to let providence, or Mrs. Garnett, take charge, at least for the moment.

But some sense of responsibility still remained. "I must send word to my cousin," she explained, "to let her know where I am."

Paper and pen were brought to her, and she penned an awkward little note to Cousin Elizabeth. To inform her of her whereabouts, Corliss summoned up the name of this crossroads inn as she had seen it from the coach at the first, the Three Crosses. She mentioned that the Garnetts were taking her home with them—in case, she thought, feeling very pleased with her own shrewdness, Mrs. Garnett and that innocent looking son of hers had evil designs on her. There was, in truth, something not quite open about them, for all their kindness.

She might have been more content if she had overheard a conversation between Mrs. Garnett and her "maid." "Mother," said the maid, "that girl's no more a servant than I am. I wonder how she came to be traveling alone. I'll wager there's a man at the bottom of it all."

Mrs. Garnett quelled her older daughter, Isabel, with a speaking glance. "If she wishes to pretend at being a maid, then it is none of our affair. Any more than you need explain to all you see how it is that our funds are not sufficient for us to travel in great state. Right now she is a girl hardly older than you, who is in trouble. And I would wish that were the same to happen to you, someone would do what we are doing."

"Ah well," said Isabel, irrepressibly, "she may be good at charades, if she plays this well at being a maid."

Corliss was helped awkwardly into the carriage, nearly swooning when her foot touched the door panel. She had the oddest sense that she was no longer herself. It was beyond belief that Corliss Hewett was riding in an unfamiliar carriage to the home of strangers. Ralph would be aghast at such an outrageous development, and she shuddered at the thought until she realized that Ralph need never know of this.

But what could she do? There was no choice. The innkeeper had demanded money at once, and she had little enough herself. Besides, if Mrs. Garnett had evil designs on Corliss, she was positive that the innkeeper was no better, and in all likelihood gave harbor to all kinds of highwaymen.

No choice at all.

Cousin Elizabeth was her only hope. In Corliss's pain-fevered thoughts, she was convinced that at all costs she must protect Ralph and the family name. But she would think about that tomorrow.

She leaned back upon the squabs, from which a faint odor of dust arose, and closed her eyes. She was in the hands of providence.

Opening her eyes briefly as the carriage swung around a corner, she caught Isabel's eye again.

The maid who wasn't a maid seemed friendly and concerned, and Corliss was warmed. I'm safe for now, she thought, and I suppose there will be a bed on which I can lie down when we get to—wherever we are going. But perhaps, if she was considered a servant, she might have to climb up to the third floor on a flight of narrow stairs . . . It did not bear thinking about.

She fell into a doze. She would not have slept as easily had she seen what was happening back at the inn.

The innkeeper, who had barely enough familiarity with the written word to keep his rude accounts, puzzled out the superscription on the letter entrusted to him to give to the next coachman going through.

"The wench said her cousin—Lady—a lady, it is all right. Wonder she didn't make it the Queen. Lady D-a-" He looked at the letter a long time before giving it up as a bad job. "Lady whatever, I'll wager, is expecting a new maid. Cousin indeed!"

With that assessment, he put the letter on the shelf to await the next northbound stage. He turned away, and did not see that the missive had slid through a crack at the back of the top shelf and found a resting place behind the undusted tankards, where it stayed, out of sight, and out of mind.

ii

Slowly, slowly, Corliss returned to the present. She had the oddest sensation of having wandered for hours, even days, in a vast, colorless wasteland. She had recognized no landmarks, no humans, merely a misty gray scene, with now and then a red flash of something she knew—without knowing how she knew—was most unpleasant.

The mist was swirling, fading. She kept her eyelids closed, wondering at the growing light coming to them from outside.

And suddenly memory returned to her with a flash.

Her eyes flew open, and she stared. At the ceiling, at first, which was no help, and then a voice spoke nearby.

"Oh good, you're awake. I thought you were never going to wake up. I was sure Mama put too many drops in your milk. But your ankle hurt so much, Mama said you must rest. How do you feel?"

Corliss stared at the girl. Surely she had seen her before? Of course, the lady's maid from the coach. "My ankle? Oh, no, it's my head," Corliss corrected her. She moved her ankle then. "It *is* my ankle. But I don't understand . . ."

"Of course you don't. But I must tell Mama you're awake. Are you hungry? I'll fetch some tea at once, and perhaps a little toast? By the way, my name's Isabel."

She was gone in a flash, leaving Corliss to marvel at the strangeness that surrounded her. A bed, a room, a girl—all these were unfamiliar. Even though she had seen Isabel before, and even begun to like her—yet surely there was much to be explained. She lay in the strange bed and bit by bit remembered.

Ralph, of course—and she was, or had been, on

her way to Cousin Elizabeth's when she fell. But
what happened next, her memory failed to explain, except to present her with the name Garnett.

Too many drops of laudanum most likely explained the fuzziness in her mind. But, she realized with gratitude, she was comfortable, and
probably, according to Isabel, would soon be fed,
and explanations could wait.

She was not left to wait long. Mrs. Garnett hurried in, followed by Isabel carrying a tray of tea
and toast. There was even, by the look of it, a
small pot of plum preserves.

"Now then, how do you feel?" said Mrs. Garnett.

Honesty burst forth. "I feel very odd. I don't
know quite where I am, nor how I got here." Nor
even who you really are, she thought but did not
say.

She looked carefully at the bearer of the tea
tray. And, she thought but did not say, you are
quite the oddest lady's maid I ever saw. Isabel was
dressed in a round morning gown the color of
primroses, and a matching ribbon held her golden
ringlets in check. Ringlets, on a lady's maid?

Corliss was thoroughly educated. Her governess
had been excellent, and had, out of affection for
the motherless child, taught her many things
beyond the required rudiments of the globe, two
foreign languages, and a solid core of good taste
and excellent manners. When she had been dismissed by Ralph, she had told Corliss, "At least I
can leave with the conviction that you can go anywhere, in any society. Not that your brother is apt
to allow an unpaid housekeeper such as you to
travel beyond the gates!"

But he had, and she had traveled this far. As

she tried to pull herself up on the pillows, pain shot through her ankle. She gasped, and then held her breath fighting down the impulse to cry out. When she could speak again, she said, tightly, "Now I remember everything." Then, as the scene of yesterday unfolded before her mind's eye, she said with a rush, "Mrs. Garnett—is that right? I owe you so much. You brought me here. . . ." A thought struck her. "I don't *think* I can walk very well today." She looked pleadingly at Mrs. Garnett. "Perhaps you could let me stay here for another day or two, until my ankle mends?"

"More like a month!" said Isabel, appearing not at all dismayed at the prospect. She plumped up the pillows behind Corliss and set the tray firmly on the invalid's knees.

"Oh, no," breathed Corliss. "A—a month? Oh, I cannot!"

Mrs. Garnett was watching her with narrowed eyes. "I think—I think, my dear, you will feel better after you have something to eat. Is the toast all right? Perhaps you would take a little broth?"

"Oh, no, ma'am, this is fine," said Corliss. "It is only that—a month? Surely I will be well before that."

"Very well, then. I'll leave Isabel here to keep you company. She'll do anything for you that you require."

Mrs. Garnett left the room. After a bit, Isabel's mischievous blue eyes turned serious. "You're running away from something, my brother Geoffrey says. Is that right?"

To gain time to frame an answer, Corliss lifted the teacup and sipped. The beverage was indeed hot and very good. Thirstily, she emptied the cup before setting it back on the tray. "What would I be running away from?"

"From a wicked step-father," said Isabel promptly, "who is forcing you to marry an evil baron, enthralled by your beauty! You are beautiful, you know."

"Nonsense!" In a moment she asked warily, not precisely remembering, "I did write a note, did I not?"

"And gave it to the landlord at the Three Crosses," agreed Isabel. "Even Three Crosses are not too many for that ungodly man." The impish glint reappeared in Isabel's eyes. "I know what's puzzling you. You can't get used to the idea that I'm only pretending to be my mother's maid. Like—"

She broke off sharply. "Like you," she had almost said, but she was sure that this young lady, while dressed in the humblest fashion possible, was no more a servant than she herself was. "Don't you ever feel like pretending? Making believe you are someone you're not?"

Sensing an answering sympathy in Corliss, who was now at work on her second piece of toast, Isabel went on, "Mama and I had to go to London on some business, and for reasons—well, no need to explain all that. But she didn't wish to take the carriage, or any of the servants. So we decided—as a huge prank, you know—to go on the public stage, and I would play Mama's abigail! It was such fun! And I fooled you, didn't I?"

Corliss, fully cognizant of the little ruses and artifices that persons of quality were sometimes forced to practice to hide their lack of funds, could only smile her sympathy. She herself had made use of some of them. And indeed, there was no shame in being a servant, or even in pretending to be one. Had she herself not told Cook that she would hire out as a kitchen maid?

"Yes," she lied generously, "you did indeed fool me. Do you do this often? For the fun of it, of course."

"Mostly for the fun of it," said Isabel, suddenly a bit wistful. "But if cousin Renfrew were a decent man. . . ."

"Who is he?"

Isabel dismissed the subject quickly. "Oh, just a family burden. By the way, you know my name is Isabel. Isabel Garnett. But we don't know yours at all!'

It was a fateful moment for Corliss, if only she had recognized it as such. But at the moment, she was only aware of an increasingly severe ache in her ankle, as well as a constricted feeling as though she were wearing a very tight stocking on that leg. There was still a lingering lethargy from the effects of the laudanum of last evening, and she longed for sleep.

However, mixed in with the laudanum seemed to be a wraith of a decision already made. Yesterday, jolting along unknown roads, she had determined that she must protect her family, although now she could not remember why.

She had known from the start that she was being treated shabbily by Ralph—public stage, no abigail, clothes more suitable to a servant than to a young lady of breeding. She had not let the circumstances concern her, since if poverty held the Hewett family in its grip, then she must make do in the best way she knew how.

But, even after all their kindness to her, she was ashamed to admit the truth. She entertained a lurking suspicion of the Garnett family, eccentric as it was. She knew her own mother, even though they might not have two sovereigns to rub together, would never have consented to Corliss's pretending to be her mother's maid.

Play-acting might well be at the root of it all—a simple diversion, harmless, and of course obviously thrifty. But Corliss, from a mixture of caution and also a wish to seem courteous to her inadvertent hostesses, did a little play-acting of her own. She would not need to think up a name suitable for a kitchen maid, as she had pretended with Cook. But there were names in plenty from novels she had read. It remained only to choose.

"Meredith." She voiced the name that had swum into her memory from an obscure novel.

"Meredith?" said Isabel doubtfully. "You are Miss Meredith?"

In for a penny. Corliss said, with as much firmness as she could over the clamor of her ankle, "Meredith Havens."

There. She had spoken, irrevocably. She was Meredith Havens—whoever that might be—and she would in all likelihood, she thought as she closed her eyes, not be Corliss Hewett again until she got to Cousin Elizabeth's.

Always supposing that Cousin Elizabeth sent her coach fare, since she had wasted the fare she did not use.

The effect of the laudanum not only had not worn off, but was reclaiming her. The last thing she heard, as she slipped into the depths of blessed sleep, was Isabel, trying out Corliss's name on her tongue, saying, "Meredith? It doesn't suit you. I'll just call you Merry."

iii

During the next two weeks, Corliss learned to answer to the name Merry, recovered to the point where she could dress and come downstairs, and became great friends with Isabel, who was only three years younger than she was.

She also became well acquainted with the other members of the family. Besides Isabel, there was Geoffrey, aged fourteen, playing at coachman the first time she had seen him, and the younger ones, generally in charge of a nursemaid named Jenny. There were three of them—Sophie, eight, Augustus, a year younger, and the baby, Jerome, still in leading-strings which he resented loudly and frequently.

And as to the Garnetts, Corliss found, to know them was to regard them with much affection.

She had graduated from her bedroom—in such a short time she was calling the pretty feminine room *hers!*—to a chair in the garden, a footstool carefully placed for her ankle by Geoffrey—"You'd make a good footman," Corliss laughed, and saw him flush with pleasure at the praise, and the family gathered around in informal posture.

It was the first time since Corliss could remember that there was a warmth of affection surrounding her—not like a smothering blanket, but like a pleasant and refreshing breeze in June. The

Garnetts asked no questions, beyond the basic one of her name. She assured them she was not running away from anything, a Bow Street runner need not be expected any instant, nor was there an irate, fire-breathing suitor on her track.

All this—the warm affection, the solid bonds, the real interest each of the family had for the others, a closeness that now, to her delight, included Corliss—all this must soon come to an end. The swelling in her ankle was going down steadily, and she could walk quite well on it. As soon as Cousin Elizabeth responded to her letter of explanation she must be on her way again to the north.

Now, having developed a complete trust in the Garnett family, she regretted her earlier caution in giving them a name not her own. If there had been an element of superstition in Corliss's thinking—in the way of postponing her future as a drudge for Cousin Elizabeth by supposing that she were for the moment someone other than Corliss—she did not recognize it.

They were a bewildering family, but an excessively happy one, and if Mrs. Garnett sometimes wore a worried little frown when she looked at her children—three boys to provide a living for and two girls who would eventually require dowries, when she clearly had barely enough to keep her own household going—her worry was not a burden on the family.

But Corliss knew that she herself was such a burden. She had used nearly her last store of coins to pay the doctor that Mrs. Garnett had summoned, so that was not a charge on the household, but surely another mouth to feed could not be welcomed forever. Yet she postponed the decision to leave. The days went on, one much like another. Corliss, hopping to a kitchen stool, helped Cook, as she had assisted Mr. Potter, but that was little enough.

She had never known a family who got so much enjoyment out of sheer existing. Every day, tea was brought out to be served under the trees. Amusingly, Isabel pretended to be parlormaid and Geoffrey often gave his impersonation of a footman. There was much laughter in the house, in the garden, in the parlor at night when they played games and charades. The younger children were a delight to Corliss. The crowning day, when she felt she was admitted to the inner heart of the family, was one she would always remember.

Little Sophie appeared solemnly before her one afternoon when she was resting her ankle in the garden. The seven-year-old was bursting with an affair of great moment. Her hands were held decorously behind her back and her expression was excessively solemn—all but her dark eyes, which were bursting with excitement.

"Come on, Augustus!" she said impatiently. "You too, Jerome."

When her brothers joined her, she took on an air of enormous import. "Now, Merry, close your eyes," she commanded. Obediently, Corliss did, feeling the sun on her hands clasped in her lap. She felt Sophie's hand turning her own wrists outward so that her palms made a cup. Then she felt hot fur placed in her hands, and her eyes flew open.

"A kitten!"

A sun-kissed tiger kitten, with a curious gaze of great intensity looking directly into Corliss's eyes.

The kitten crawled up her bodice until it could
bump its nose against hers.

"It thinks you're its mother!" cried Sophie with
delight "It belongs to you now. My mother says it's
a girl cat, and you have to name it."

Curiously, the small incident took on weighty
meaning. I've bumped the noses, so to speak, of
all the Garnetts. Almost I could believe that I've
been adopted, like this kitten, she thought, almost—
tempering her affection for them with a touch of
wariness, lest this lovely interlude crash to bits.

Sophie was clamoring, "What's her name, Merry?"

Corliss's answer was automatic. This was a lively
sprite of a kitten. "Miranda, of course."

There was much that the Garnett establishment
had in common with Hewett Manor. Corliss knew
now that the Garnetts too possessed skimpy money
resources, which probably accounted for the lack
of many social activities, the general air of falling
gently backward rather than making solid progress ahead. All these combined to make an atmosphere that felt comfortable to her. But the Garnett
family had something that Ralph Hewett would
never have, indeed, would not even recognize it as
something to be desired. That was a good nature,
a making of great happiness from small beginnings, and Corliss's little tiger kitten was a symbol
of that philosophy.

Not only were there to be enjoyed the endless
pranks played by a curious kitten, the arched back
and the improbably high sideways jumps. There
was also the frequent clawing up her skirt to find
a resting place in her lap. From there, Miranda
often pulled herself up until she could bump noses
again with her new mistress—an activity that gave
them both a great deal of satisfaction.

However, with the recollection of the differences between the household she had grown up in and this one where she had so fortuitously landed after her accident, came the stern realization that she must move on. She could do nothing to repay the Garretts for their help and comfort, for their generous affection and their unstinting sharing of their substance with her. She could not repay them, and she must move on, to Cousin Elizabeth in the wilds of northern England.

If she were still welcome at Dacre Hall, after her failure to arrive.

It seemed odd that there was no answer to Corliss's note. Cousin Elizabeth was now informed of the reasons for the delay, and it was worrying that she had had no answer. But perhaps someone must go to the Three Crosses to pick up the mail, and most likely no one had taken the time to do so.

She must be sure that, whenever someone went to town, inquiry would be made on her behalf.

It was just the following day that the subject of the mails arose. Supplies for the household, too, were needed and Geoffrey was dispatched to the village at the crossroads to accomplish the errands.

"Would you not like to ride into town with Geoffrey?" asked Mrs. Garnett. "I am persuaded you find things rather dull here, although you are much too civil to say so!"

Geoffrey set off at a fast pace down the drive, clearly, considering the flourish with which he drove, seeing in himself a notable whip. Doubtless he would have cast all others into the shade, had they been forced to compete on the same terms—

those of driving an ancient curricle and a horse more often hitched up to a farm wagon.

At the Three Crossroads, Geoffrey dropped to the ground, handing the reins to her. "Do you mind, Merry? I don't trust any of these fellows here to hold him."

Corliss didn't mind. Indeed, considering the inclination of this horse to run away as remote to the point of impossibility, she said mischievously, "Shall I walk him after ten minutes?"

Taking her jest seriously, Geoffrey said, "Well, I don't expect to be gone that long."

"Don't forget to ask if there is a letter for me, please."

There was only one letter waiting to be picked up, and that was for Mrs. Garnett. Nothing for Corliss.

Corliss was low in her mind. She felt as though all the walls were closing in on her. There was no place for Corliss to go. And she could not remain here.

But she was not to leave yet, for Mrs. Garnett begged her to stay. "My mother has written that she is coming for a visit," she explained in tones of doom. "You must help me keep her busy! She has the most abominable habit of interfering!"

Four

i

Lady Jarman bore a resemblance to her daughter, Mrs. Garnett, in the way a hatchet resembles a penknife. Where Mrs. Garnett was kind, Lady Jarman was sensible. Where Mrs. Garnett was gentle and vague, Lady Jarman got her own way.

It took Corliss a few days before she discovered Lady Jarman's technique for prevailing against all opposition. She quite simply did not hear any objections. She was most civil, bending an attentive eye to an opponent, bending forward as though to listen with every appearance of fascinated interest, and then, when it was her turn to speak again, simply going on from where she had left off.

In a way, Corliss admired her. She herself could not do it, or at least, her young years would not give her the same privileges as Lady Jarman had earned. How satisfying it must be to see all your wishes carried out at once, rather than waiting upon events to unfold, and perhaps not even the way one would like.

Although Corliss had not yet seen the interference Mrs. Garnett had prophesied, Lady Jarman had certainly effected change in her daughter's household

"Time to stop grieving for a man who could not even provide for his family," Lady Jarman pointed out. "This place is going downhill without brakes! Something has to be done!"

"But what?" asked Mrs. Garnett quietly. Her mother only snorted. Nonetheless, in Lady Jarman's presence the family stepped a little more quickly, spoke with a bit more preciseness. The days when the Garnetts and Corliss idled away the hours in the sunlit garden were regrettably gone.

Lady Jarman's first interview with Corliss had not been reassuring. "Meredith!" Lady Jarman sniffed in a most ladylike way. "An odd name for a girl—sounds like a Minerva Press heroine."

How very true! Corliss hoped she was not blushing.

"And I never heard of the Havens family. Yorkshire, I believe you said?"

Actually, Corliss had very carefully *not* said where her mythical family seat was, to the Garnetts, who had not asked, nor to Lady Jarman who had, more than once. She could have her choice, she realized with amusement, a ruined castle in Scotland, an old monastery, reclaimed, in Yorkshire . . .

This time she offered no resistance. "Quite right, Lady Jarman."

She could not tell whether Lady Jarman approved of her or not. She believed darkly that if the truth were to come out, Lady Jarman would not only banish her from her daughter's house, but might well, so indignant would she be, escort Corliss right to the stage and see that she got on it.

Fortunately, Lady Jarman lost interest in her, at least for the moment. She had a matter of far greater moment on her mind, and she informed Mrs. Garnett at once of her concern.

"You know, I have always said that Garnett's father treated you abominably. That ridiculous way of handling his money. One could be sure it was a man's mind that thought up such a mish-mash."

"Not George's father—his grandfather."

"No matter. Tying up all that money just because he had such a bad experience with marriage! Well, after all, what could one expect if one married a wench right off the stage at Covent Garden! Of course his marriage went sour. But is that any reason to punish Geoffrey and Isabel?"

Not to say Sophie and Augustus and little Jerome, soon to be out of leading strings, thought Mrs. Garnett. Or even me!

Corliss knew nothing of the Garnett forebears. She knew there were several oil portraits in an upstairs corridor, but they were dark with age and hung in such poor light that she could not make out any features clearly. Now, realizing that a frank discussion of family affairs impended, she rose to excuse herself. She had reached the door before she was stopped by a hail from Lady Jarman.

"You there, Meredith! Come back here."

"I do not wish," said Corliss with considerable dignity, "to intrude on private family matters."

Lady Jarman regarded her with speculative eye. She saw a sweet-faced, good-natured girl of excellent manners, and doubtless of sufficient breeding to make feasible the plan that had spring to her mind all of a piece, as Athena leaped from Jove's brow. Let us hope, she thought, that the girl, besides being really quite pretty, is also biddable.

Lady Jarman was not quite sure just what the girl's position was in the household, but she did not need to clutter up her lovely plan with details.

"Nonsense!" she rode over Corliss's protest. "How old are you, my dear?"

Feeling that a bit of maturity might stand her in good stead at the moment, Corliss added six months to the truth. "Twenty, ma'am."

"Twenty," repeated Lady Jarman in a reflective tone. "Not too giddy." And near enough to putting on a spinster's cap, since I haven't heard of any marriage prospects for either this one or Isabel since my arrival. Aloud, she added, "Just come back and sit there in that chair. I want you to hear all this. Now Margaret, have you told this child how old Renfrew's will ran?"

"No, Mama, why should I? It is not something for Meredith to worry about. Indeed, I do not understand why you do not let her go. She will be bored indeed!"

"I think not *bored*, precisely," said Lady Jarman with a sly look. 'Young lady—Meredith, is it? We'll have to change that. Such a really *common* name! I've a tale to tell you that will add to your understanding of men. Idiots, all of them. You let me know the minute you get bored, do you hear?"

Corliss, feeling like a leaf suddenly adrift on a swift-running stream, said, politely, "Yes, ma'am."

"Idiots, all of them," she repeated. "Old Renfrew, Garnett's grandfather, was no exception. In his dotage, he married a cheap little actress who took his fancy. She took everything else that she could carry, as well. Why he didn't just set her up in a flat, I never could see."

"Mama!"

"Don't pretend you don't know these things, Margaret. George wasn't all that—"

"*Mama!*" said Mrs. Garnett, a surprisingly firm note in her voice. "Meredith does not care—"

"But she has heard nothing yet." Lady Jarman addressed Corliss directly. "As he must, the old man left his entailed fortune, which was enough to buy out the Indies, to his grandson, Douglas Renfrew. He also left a modest fortune that was not entailed to young Douglas on the condition that he not marry."

"Not marry? But—"

"The entail was solid, and of course there must be heirs. But the moment young Renfrew announces his betrothal in the *Gazette*, this so-called modest fortune must be turned over to Margaret here."

Lady Jarman eyed Corliss to ascertain the effect her words had on the girl. But Corliss was merely puzzled.

"That seems like an idiotic thing to do. Of course, he will marry. How else will there be an heir?"

"Very true. But the old man was just *mean*. He simply wanted to inform the world as to his feelings about women. And it's an outrage that leaves Margaret with no money to speak of, because who would have expected George to go out in a thunderstorm and stand for shelter under a great oak tree. You can see the stump from the rise beyond the stable."

"But could not the young man—Douglas Renfrew you said?—simply turn over that income to Mrs. Garnett?"

"Certainly, he could. He has power of disposal of that money. But of course the man's been fighting with Wellington on the Peninsula, and probably does not know what is going on here."

Mrs. Garnett spoke, and there was an unaccustomed note of bitterness in her voice. "I'm sure he knows. I went to London to see his man of business. In truth, that was the errand from which I was returning when I met Meredith on the stagecoach."

"Stagecoach?" repeated Lady Jarman ominously.

"Well, of course, Mama. I could not ride in my own coach, don't you see, since I don't regard it as safe for a long journey."

"But your maid? You surely didn't take that ninny with you!"

"No, indeed, Grandmama," said Isabel bravely. "She took me. I make a very good maid, you know. Even Merry was fooled! As a matter of fact, I thought she too was a servant, but I was wrong!"

Lady Jarman fanned herself quickly. "I cannot take this in. Margaret, you went to London on your own? You traveled on the public stage? I never! And you, Isabel, pretended to be an abigail?" Her own family's derelictions stunned her. She turned to Corliss. "And Meredith, I am sure that my granddaughter is mistaken. Surely you too were not play-acting at being an abigail!"

Corliss was not quite sure what the proper answer might be. However, the last refuge lay in telling the truth, so she did. Up to a point, of course. She was on her way to a new position as a companion. Now she was abundantly justified in having given another name, for Lady Jarman's horror at such breaches of convention was appalling to see.

She cried out, when she could find voice again, "Traveling without an abigail, and so young. Totally ineligible! What could your family have been thinking of!"

"I cannot say, Lady Jarman," said Corliss sturdily, "for I have none." This, while not literally accurate, was true enough.

The play of emotions over Lady Jarman's strong features entertained Corliss for a moment. The woman could not approve of a world which contained such breaches of decorum. But in a moment, her horror was transmuted into speculation. "No family? Well now, Providence is watching out for us. Margaret, do I understand from your wretched expression that you did not receive satisfaction from Renfrew's man?"

"He told me," said Mrs. Garnett with remembered resentment, "that Colonel Renfrew had more important affairs to think about than a destitute female relative who had no possible claim on him."

"Didn't you explain about the reversion?"

"He knew about it. Oh, yes, he knew. And he took great pleasure in turning me down. I was so ashamed!"

"Well," said Lady Jarman after a long silence, "that alters the situation. We must get young Douglas married off at once. Or betrothed."

"You mean an announcement in the *Gazette* would be sufficient?" asked Corliss. "He doesn't actually have to marry?"

"Not in the least. And I should not think anyone would want to marry him. For you must know that the recent *on-dit* in town is that Colonel Renfrew has been sadly wounded, or is ill with the ague, or something—but at any rate, he is returning to England. And I think we must make it our business to see that he is betrothed before he dies."

"Of course," said Isabel impulsively, "he could not be betrothed afterward."

"Mind your tongue, Isabel," said her grandmother, even though a twinkle appeared in her old eyes. "You might have to go out as an abigail in truth, if we don't succeed in our scheme."

A note in her mother's voice caught Mrs. Garnett's attention. "Scheme?" she echoed.

Corliss found her breath tight in her chest. She was beginning to take the measure of this formidable old woman, and if Lady Jarman were scheming, then it might be well for those nearest to seek shelter. Corliss made a motion as if to rise.

"Meredith," said Lady Jarman, "do you possess any more fashionable gowns than that sad muslin? I thought not." She looked intently at Corliss. "If I had the dressing of you, my child, I would wager the Regent himself could not resist you. You have the makings of a great beauty, but a bit of style would not come amiss. Perhaps a fortnight of hard work—"

"I do not think, Lady Jarman—"

"Quite right, Meredith. Let me do the thinking." Lady Jarman's brow furrowed.

"Havens," she mused. "No, we'll have to change that name to one less vulnerable in case of investigation."

"Lady Jarman—" Corliss began again, only to be interrupted ruthlessly.

"We'll talk about it later," said Lady Jarman.

"Talk about what? Ma'am, I confess I have grave doubts—"

"Very well, Miss Meredith Havens. I perceive that you are full of questions. Let me pose one to you first. My daughter and her family rescued you from an unpleasant situation, is that correct?"

"Yes, Lady Jarman."

"And they have kept you here at their charge until you are quite well? And you have no family?"

It was all too true, thought Corliss, feeling an unkind fate approaching inexorably, not even bothering to steal upon her.

"How do you plan to repay their kindness?" demanded Lady Jarman.

A chorus of protest arose. "But Mama," said Mrs. Garnett, "there's no need—"

Isabel joined her. "We love her. She's one of the family!"

"Very well," said Lady Jarman ruthlessly. "Then let her act like one."

Corliss at last made herself heard. "And how shall I do that, Lady Jarman?"

"Very simple," said Lady Jarman, sensing victory. "Simply get yourself betrothed to Colonel Douglas Renfrew."

When Corliss escaped at last from the arguments that swirled around her head, from the tumult and the sound of a family for once in strong disagreement with each other, and gained the quiet harbor of her room, she sank into a chair next to the window and closed her eyes. Her head pounded in remembered rhythm with the

Garnetts who leaped to her rescue. Isabel was—at least at first—shocked at the very idea of pursuing a stranger with the purpose of marrying him.

"Not marriage, child," Lady Jarman pointed out, "Simply a formal betrothal. Meredith can cry off the moment the necessary financial arrangements have been put in train."

"Loathsome!" cried Mrs. Garnett. "Meredith owes us nothing."

"Not even gratitude? Affection?" inserted Lady Jarman, slyly.

But gradually, Corliss detected a subtle shift in the stands of the various disputants. It was clear to Corliss that Isabel, perhaps the weakest link in the chain of opposition, was struggling against a vision of her own—and not fighting successfully. A Season in London for her was at stake, and a chance at a good marriage. Even Geoffrey, arriving late, drawn by the sounds of raised voices, mentioned a term or two at Cambridge.

And Corliss knew that there was Sophia to come, and Augustus, who must be given a chance in the church or in the army, and even small Jerome must be provided for.

She had thought her life had taken a severe turn for the worse when she had boarded the stage on her way to Cousin Elizabeth's. How fortunate she had been to sprain her ankle, she had thought secretly, and be taken care of by the Garnetts.

Now—as Ralph was wont to say—she had to pay the piper. And what a price the piper was exacting! Even supposing—and she had a strong feeling that supposing was about to turn into reality— she was able to find Colonel Renfrew, wherever he was lying at the point of death, how could she then charm him into offering for her? What kind of man was he? A gnarled, military martinet, pompous, grizzled . . .

No, no she could not do it.

But what else could she do?

Galvanized by the need to find an escape, she leaped to her feet and began to rummage in her bandbox. She set aside her prayer book, her combs, her toilet articles, laying them at random on the bed. Then she found what she was looking for.

She picked up a small cloisonné box, given her by her mother. Inside the box was her very last store of small coins against the journey. She laid them out on the palm of her hand and counted them. Enough to get her, possibly, to Cousin Elizabeth's. But what then? Cousin Elizabeth clearly did not want her, for she had sent no word of any kind. Corliss might have to buy passage on the roof of the coach, but she shuddered at the impropriety, not to say danger, of such an endeavor.

There was, of course, carefully wrapped in a linen cloth, the brooch of her mother's. Perhaps she could sell it?

She would certainly have to part with the brooch, no matter how agonizing such a decision must be. Surely her mother would not want her to embark upon such a questionable pursuit of an unsuspecting gentleman!

But then, said her other self judiciously, would my mother have wanted me to ride in a stagecoach across England to a cousin who has no interest in me and enter into a life of wretchedness? There was no doubt in Corliss's mind but what going to Lady Dacre's, and becoming a small and neglected cog in that household, was not a happy prospect.

Perhaps there was something to be said for Lady Jarman's plan—not a lot, but something.

ii

At the same moment as Corliss stood alone in her borrowed bedroom, holding her mother's brooch in her hand as though to receive a kind of reassurance, perhaps even advice, from the mere touch of it, across the country at Scarborough her name had just been mentioned.

Scarborough, at this season, held the charm of full summer tempered by a cool wind from the North Sea. Most invigorating, Lady Dacre was wont to say, all the while taking great care to avoid exposure to the freshening breeze.

Quite the equivalent of Bath, Lady Dacre thought, as she moved toward the assembly rooms on her first excursion of the day. Habit played a great part in the enjoyment of Scarborough—habit, and the self-deceiving notion that the worse a dose of medicine tasted, the more efficacious its results.

But of course, any change from Lady Dacre's usual sedentary habits must result in at least the illusion of better health, and so it was this morning.

"Towne," she said to her companion, a few steps behind her as was proper, "I believe the waters are doing me a good deal of benefit. I shall surely be able to keep up with dear Corliss next April."

"Next April, my lady?"

"Of course, Towne. Dear Fanny's daughter must have a Season, even if I fall invalid from the pace. A fast one, Towne, but most enjoyable." She sighed reminiscently. "If one is young."

"I wonder at your taking the trouble, my lady," said Towne in a dark tone. "You know nothing about the girl, as I see it. You know how you dislike the noise of the city, and all the scurrying around."

And that, thought Towne, was putting a good face on it, for what she meant was that her mistress was indolent, even lazy, and stirred herself for nothing but her own comfort.

Lady Dacre's well-known lethargy was Towne's commission to rule the household in her own way, using Lady Dacre's name often in vain as her authority. In this persuasion, Towne was well off the mark. Completely insensitive to the ideas and thoughts of those around her, she believed that she held Dacre Hall in the hollow of her hand. She recognized no symptoms of coming rebellion, or even of incipient treachery biding its time before bursting into full and open flame.

Her mistress stepped with more liveliness as she approached her destination. Towne lengthened her stride to keep pace.

"I do hope," said Lady Dacre, "that Corliss does not consider me rude because I am not at home to welcome her. Flint will certainly see that she is comfortable."

Glancing sidelong at her maid's dour expression, she added, "Pray, Towne, do not try to set my mind against the girl. It will not do at all."

"Of course not, my lady. A sweet young miss, I am sure."

Neither of them considered that statement as truth.

Later, settled in comfort in a favorite chair from which she could see everyone who entered the public rooms, Lady Dacre was agreeably surprised to catch sight of an old acquaintance coming toward her. The journey took some time, since the room was already crowded even at that early hour.

"Arabella Childress!" Lady Dacre greeted her with pleasure. "Do sit down beside me! It's been a long time since we had a comfortable coze."

After some time spent in gently competitive boasting, in the main about their interesting daily activities, Lady Dacre produced her trump card.

"You remember my dear cousin Fanny? Fanny Monteith, she was."

"A sad case," affirmed Lady Childress. "Married badly, didn't she?"

Lady Dacre explained the unhappy rift between herself and Fanny, and now the welcome healing of that quarrel with the expected arrival of Fanny's daughter, Corliss.

"What's young Hewett have in mind, Elizabeth? You know, if he is old Sir Gervase's son, he's got some scheme in mind, mark my words. He's the only one left, isn't he? I have no idea what's happened to that family."

"All the better," said Lady Dacre stoutly. "He will not call the girl back home, interfering with my plans for her. Arabella, I shall so enjoy her!"

Arabella Childress was a woman of some acumen. She knew that Elizabeth Dacre was at heart an excessively kind soul, and was more often than not to view her geese as first-class swans. But she could remember the Elizabeth Monteith of years gone by, a sprightly, merry young lady, good-natured and gentle. Any girl would the better for Elizabeth's tutelage.

Arabella, however, had some doubts. She did not know she had spoken aloud until she noticed the other's horrified expression.

"Arabella," said Lady Dacre decisively, "I will not believe that Corliss could take after her dreadful father. In fact, Ralph wrote that she was a quiet, biddable girl who would do her mother credit, although I must say in that case, she has more sense than her mother. But I do wish he had been more precise in his letter. I expected him to tell me when his coach would arrive—"

"His coach? Very generous of him, *and* out of character, I should think. I remember his father— But that does not matter any more."

"How else would she come, Arabella? He would send her in his coach, of course, along with her maid. It is not to be thought of that he would not take the greatest care of her. I wonder who he might send with her as a chaperone? She has no relatives, but perhaps a governess? To think," she ended sadly, "that only Corliss and I are left of all the Monteiths. So many changes, as the old families die out or lose influence. Even the Hewetts were an honorable line, though so obscure that I doubt anyone now remembers them, except you and me, perhaps. Ah, things change, and not for the better, either."

In spite of her remark to Arabella Childress, Lady Dacre was not at all perturbed not to have some recent word from Corliss. The girl's half-brother had made arrangements for Corliss to travel to Yorkshire, so of course she would arrive.

Lady Dacre had left detailed instructions as to
which room Corliss was to have, where to house
her abigail, and the proper arrangements to be
made for Ralph's servants and cattle before they
were sent on their way back to Hewett Manor.
Flint had accepted his orders with an impassive
expression. He would have managed everything
on his own, as his mistress well knew, and very
well, too.

By now, thought Elizabeth Dacre, doubtless
Corliss had arrived. It did not occur to her to send
to inquire as to the fact. What could happen to a
young lady properly chaperoned, safeguarded by
several servants who were in all likelihood bearing
arms, and traveling in her brother's private coach?

iii

At that moment, Corliss was feeling that, much
like sheep being herded into the fold, she was
being nudged into a situation she was not entirely
sure about. She was, moreover, puzzled by the
lack of response to the letter she had sent Cousin
Elizabeth from the inn, when she was first injured. Even a scolding missive from the cousin she
did not know would have meant *something*—even
as little as simply that her existence was acknowledged. As it was, she was so thoroughly adopted
by the Garnett family—and a happy arrangement
it had been, until Lady Jarman arrived with her
mad plan—that she had all but lost the Corliss
Hewett part of herself.

She answered readily now to her new name, Meredith Havens—

Still holding her mother's brooch in her hand, almost as though it provided an indestructible link to her identity, she stopped short. Her hand tightened convulsively over the brooch, and her mistake came clearly and vividly to her mind.

Of course there was no word from Cousin Elizabeth.

How could there be? No one at the inn would know how to deliver a missive addressed to Corliss Hewett. She must get to the inn and make inquiry— but how could she manage the journey without giving herself away?

The answer was clear. Geoffrey!

She remembered that Lady Jarman had asked him to travel to the village on some errands—to pick up her own letters, among other things. Corliss must accompany him. Once at the inn, she would think of some ploy to remove him, so that she could speak privately to the innkeeper.

She rushed downstairs to catch Geoffrey before he left.

Lady Jarman stood in the hall, giving what were probably last-minute instructions to Geoffrey. She glanced up when she heard Corliss on the stairs.

"Have you made up your mind to help out in the family business?" Her tone carried an accusing overtone. She could as well have said clearly, "The Garnetts took you in and you owe them a great deal."

That was true enough, but Corliss's thoughts were full of her new idea—that there was a missive waiting for Corliss, under her real name.

"Please, Lady Jarman," said Corliss, not answering directly. "I should like to go into town with Geoffrey. Will you wait till I get my shawl, Geoffrey?"

Lady Jarman said, "Of course he will."

Corliss turned and ran upstairs, too quickly to hear Lady Jarman's remark to Geoffrey. "I expect you to say the right things to Meredith. You know how important this scheme is to us all."

iv

Obediently, Geoffrey, driving the cart and trying desperately to pretend that he sat competently on the seat of a dashing phaeton, did his best.

"My cousin, Colonel Renfrew, you know, is the meanest man alive. Why, if we had that income that should have come to us in the beginning, he'd never miss it. Wealthy as a nabob, my grandmother says."

"But is the money really yours?" asked Corliss. She was heartily weary of hearing about the detestable Colonel Renfrew, especially when she had discovered that only Lady Jarman had met him, for above all she must be considered as a prejudiced observer. Even Mrs. Garnett, it developed, did not know him.

Even so, she suspected darkly that she would before long find herself dancing to Lady Jarman's melody. But while there was a chance that Cousin Elizabeth had written to her, even if she did not enclose funds for her passage north, Corliss could not agree. She had those few sovereigns secreted for desperate circumstances. She could, if pushed to the wall, buy passage at least to somewhere where she might find work.

As though she were lacking in understanding, Geoffrey explained that excessively odd will once again.

The entail, which was the source of the vast funds that Geoffrey spoke of, could not be touched. But the announcement of the betrothal of Douglas Renfrew in the *Gazette* was sufficient to alter the prospects of the Garnett family. A tidy sum, said Geoffrey, and then in a burst of honesty said, "Actually, it's not all that much. But without it, there's no dowry for Isabel, and I can't go to Cambridge, to say nothing of the rest of them. And my mother won't be able to afford another maid—she's saving all the money we have for us, you see."

"An infamous arrangement!"

"Of course. But there's no changing it," said Geoffrey simply.

Unless, thought Corliss, Lady Jarman prevails. I don't want to do it, thought Corliss rebelliously. Why can't I simply be honest, and use my own name, not get embroiled in make-believe?

Corliss was learning, as others have learned, that it is not the lie in itself that causes the trouble. It is the subsequent lies that become necessary to cover up and support the first lie that lead to disaster.

The first lie—that had to be climbing on the stagecoach and allowing the other passengers to consider her as a maid. And that, to be honest, was not Corliss's lie, but rather Ralph's parsimony. But, she thought as they pulled into the yard of the coaching inn, she had certainly compounded the original sin, and she would consider herself well out of this moil if no disaster fell on her head.

Perhaps, her desperate optimism convinced her, in only moments she would hold Cousin Elizabeth's letter in her hands.

Geoffrey delayed in the yard, giving her time enough to lift her skirts and hurry into the dingy interior of the inn where she had left her letter to be sent to Lady Dacre.

"Letter?" said the innkeeper. "What name?"

"Corliss Hewett," she said in a low voice, glancing over her shoulder to be sure that Geoffrey was out of earshot. "There must be a letter for—for that name!"

He shook his head slowly. Really, these people who considered themselves the quality gave more trouble than the local inhabitants. For one, you could not give way to the contempt they inspired, for you might find yourself in difficulties. But at least you could answer sullenly, and the landlord took full advantage of that privilege.

Corliss turned away with tears standing in her eyes, hardly aware of the strong smell of spilled spirits and unwashed landlord, and stumbled blindly into Geoffrey, who was arriving at that moment.

"What's amiss?" he demanded, glaring with fourteen-year-old anger at the landlord, the most likely source of trouble for Corliss.

"N-nothing," she said. "Oh, j-just nothing!"

She stumbled out into the daylight. Geoffrey, not knowing quite how to wipe the knowing look from the landlord's face, contented himself with demanding Lady Jarman's parcels.

While the landlord searched for the parcels, Geoffrey had time to look around him. There, on the shelf behind the bar, the shelf containing the unwashed tankards, he caught sight of the corner of a missive. It had clearly slid down behind the shelf, and was caught out of sight until most likely a recent removal of one of the tankards jostled it loose.

Geoffrey recognized it. It was the letter that Merry had written that day when she fell and sprained her ankle. It had never been sent!

She was crying, he thought, because she had received no reply to the letter that, instead of reaching its destination, had rested hidden in the taproom of the Three Crosses. If she had received an answer, Geoffrey had no doubt, she would be on her way to somewhere else without delay.

But then, she would not fall in with his grandmother's scheme.

He knew he should tell Corliss what had happened to her letter, and also give the landlord what he deserved and demand that the letter be forwarded at once.

But then, Colonel Douglas Renfrew—now, according to Lady Jarman, desperately wounded and in danger of a premature death— would never be induced to share his money.

The struggle in Geoffrey's bosom was short. Laden with Lady Jarman's parcels, he followed Corliss out into the inn yard. Thoroughly stifling his conscience, he said, "I think we've finished here, Merry. Let me help you up."

v

Corliss's spirits sank lower the nearer they came
to the house. No answer from Cousin Elizabeth,
who quite clearly did not care whether she, Corliss,
lived or died. Even if she had not seen fit to
answer Corliss's own letter, she could at least have
informed Ralph that his half-sister was adrift somewhere in England with no money and no resources.

The outcome of her brooding was simple. Nobody cared what happened to her. She had only
the Garnetts—kind, muddle-minded, happy-dis-
positioned—on whom to rely.

There was no way out. It was clear that Ralph
had washed his hands of her. What kind of brother
would send her out alone on a public stage? Not a
loving brother, that was certain. And her mother's
cousin, Lady Dacre, was surprisingly no better.

No way out— But perhaps there was.

These two were the only relatives she knew about.
But perhaps there were relations that she did not
know about? How could she find out? She remembered that in the Garnett library there was a
shelf of country histories. Written mostly by par-
sons, particularly those attached to great families
whose only duties were presiding at Sunday services and making up a table of whist when required, the volumes were for the most part dusty
in style and exhaustive in detail. Fanning the small
ember of hope that remained to her, she sought
refuge and information in the dim library.

For preference, her mother's family. Monteith
. . . Here it was. "Elizabeth, m. Gervase Dacre, 9th

bt., etc." And that was all. Not another Monteith in the history, at least still alive. A thought quickly struck her—perhaps Cousin Elizabeth had died in the interval between her letter to Ralph and Corliss's own letter to her! She caught her breath. It was certainly possible, and would explain the continuing silence.

In that case, she had only Ralph, and whatever other Hewetts still lived.

She skimmed quickly. Hewett . . . A long list of her unillustrious ancestors, all gone now. Her father's marriage to Fanny Monteith, her own birth, Corliss Margaret Elizabeth Hewett . . ."

And no more Hewetts.

The last door had closed—even slammed—in her face. She might as well be Meredith Havens, who as far as Corliss knew not only had no relations, but did not herself exist. For as to that, she would be hard put to prove that Corliss Hewett existed.

She had gone to the window to get better light on the fine print of the county history, and now she moved back to sit in one of the shabby chairs. The book lay open in her lap, and absently she pressed it open with her hand while she lost herself in thought.

The choice was clear. She could fall in with Lady Jarman's mad plan, or she could make her way to another town and find work for which she had not the slightest aptitude, and be alone again. If she acceded to Lady Jarman's persuasion—and it was easy to discern from where stemmed the slightly lunatic activities of the Garnett family—then she would have at least the company of these people she loved. And she did not really have to marry any stranger.

She had not thought clearly about the gentleman involved. How hard it was not to think of him as "the prey!" However disagreeable he might be, she must only accept his offer, wait till he put the announcement in the journals, and then cry off.

For the first time, she thought beyond the apparently insurmountable barriers between going on to Cousin Elizabeth and becoming yet again someone else and playing a role as an eligible female on the Marriage Mart. Now, the inevitable complications came to her like a tidal bore, inexorable, overwhelming. How could she get him to offer for her? If he had that much wealth, it was to be expected that he would be pursued by many a belle and her mother. Why would he be attracted to her more than any other?

When Lady Jarman, Mrs. Garnett on her heels, came into the room, Corliss looked at them with dull eyes. Lady Jarman read the answer she expected, and said so. "At last you've made up your mind, Meredith. Good! You won't regret it. Now then, we have much to do. I wonder about all those gowns in your trunks in the attic, Margaret. We must get them down and see what can be of use. I know I spent a good penny or two on them when you were married."

Lady Jarman's lips closed firmly. And a waste of money that was! she added to herself.

"Can that Miss whatever her name is finish a wardrobe for Meredith in a week?"

"If she does not have other work."

"Of course, she won't have other work. We had

best have her here in the house until she's finished. Now then, Meredith, we must rid you of that most unsuitable name. I do not know a Havens family, and we must be careful to make sure that no busybody can look up your antecedents and not find any."

"My family—" began Corliss.

"Give me a little time, Meredith." Lady Jarman picked up the book that had slid unheeded from Corliss's lap. "We must not hurry over this." She opened the book she held while Mrs. Garnett crossed the room to sit near Corliss.

"My dear, I am so sorry you have been swept up in this scheme. It was the farthest thing from my mind when I brought you here."

"I know," said Corliss. "And from mine. But you have been so kind to me. I truly don't know what I would have done without you. And—" She glanced at Lady Jarman, rapt over the book. "She can be very persuasive, can she not?"

"Oh, she can indeed. And often to my great regret."

Lady Jarman spoke, and Corliss felt her heart stop for a long time before it began tentatively to beat again.

"Corliss!" Lady Jarman cried. "Corliss Hewett! Just the right name!"

"How. . . !" Corliss's voice died in her throat.

Lady Jarman slapped the open book with one hand.

"Here's your new name! Nobody left in the family. One son, it says, first marriage. Probably dead by now, at least I've never heard of him. And a daughter of the second marriage—Corliss Hewett." She looked triumphantly at Corliss. "That's you.

Family on record, but nobody to make any trouble. Just the thing!"

Corliss could not even think. They had found her out, and yet they hadn't. She was Corliss, but now she was to be christened Corliss again—it was all the worst muddle she could ever have imagined. She swallowed, but still her voice caught in her throat. Nor was there anything she could say!

Lady Jarman and Mrs. Garnett conversed over her head and she did not hear them, except for a word or two. Lady Jarman was saying, "First we'll go to Bath for a fortnight."

"Bath?"

"We must get Meredith—I mean, Corliss—accustomed to society gradually."

"But why Bath?"

"You're right, Margaret. We'll need an excuse, of course. You need to take the waters, that's it. You are not at all well."

Margaret protested. "I never felt better in my life!"

"Do you mean," said her mother ominously, "that you are not willing to pretend to a little *malaise* in order to get your children—your five children—settled in life?"

"Of course, I am," sighed Margaret Garnett. "I often wonder why affairs do not march in a straightforward fashion, Mama. Does your mind always work like a corkscrew?"

"Not always, Margaret. But you will recall that you already attempted the straight approach, and all you gained were insults from Renfrew's man. It's time for a devious plan." She thought, and added, "And help from Providence."

Providence—the word caught Corliss's ear. She

could agree, she thought ruefully, that Providence was already taking a hand in the affair. How else could one account for Lady Jarman's choice of that one name to fit the role she was to play?

Oh, yes, she would play that role, she knew. After the last few minutes, and that dreadful moment when she heard her own name sounding like a trumpet call to arms, she knew she was totally enmeshed in the scheme.

She must agree. But why did she think she could hear the sound of a trap snapping shut?

Five

i

Bath had to be seen to be believed, thought Corliss, setting out for a walk with Isabel a reluctant two steps behind her in the role of her faithful abigail, but, unservant-like, prone to making unseemly comments sufficiently loud to reach Corliss's ear.

They had been in Bath for almost a week now, in rooms that Lady Jarman had rented in New King Street. Mrs. Garnett, to keep up the pretense that the excursion to Bath was on her account, went each day to the Pump room for the daily ritual.

"One glass of that undrinkable water I will take," she told her mother, "for appearance's sake. But not the prescribed three. I would be ill in truth."

Most visitors, it was well known, mortified the flesh by taking three glasses of warm spa water in the morning before partaking of a congenial breakfast in the Pump Room, where sooner or later, it was said, one met all one's friends and acquaintances. Then there was excellent music to listen to, shopping to do if one had funds, promenades to be taken to the magnificent Perpendicular cathedral or along Wood's graceful Royal Crescent.

Corliss lost herself in wonder at the alteration in her circumstances that had taken place in the last six weeks.

It was now mid-August, and there were a number of valetudinarians in residence. Lady Jarman and the Garnetts had come to Bath for mixed reasons. The first, ostensible one, of course, was to restore Mrs. Garnett to blooming health. The second Lady Jarman shared only with her daughter.

Lady Jarman realized full well that she was hazarding everything, both her own comfortable income and the future of her daughter and her family, on a young miss of whose antecedents and breeding she knew nothing. The girl Meredith Havens, while her manners were charming and her demeanor spoke of excellent breeding, yet was without family or known background. In truth, Lady Jarman had no very high hopes of a girl found traveling alone on a public stage with only a small trunk and a bandbox. However, once the all-important betrothal was announced, young Miss Havens might disappear into Yorkshire or wherever she really had been traveling.

Unheard of! thought Lady Jarman. If she were an orphan, would she not have said so? She had stated most firmly that she had no family. But that did not of necessity mean *no family*. It meant only, as far as Lady Jarman was concerned, no one with an immediate urge to interfere in her own plans.

Mark my words, Lady Jarman said, but only to herself, there's in all likelihood a story behind the girl's existence that might well fill a Minerva novel. But if the girl would only behave herself, and not run off on a convenient stagecoach, long enough to get that selfish Renfrew in her toils—not wed, but merely betrothed publicly—Lady Jarman would not care what scandal might break over their heads later. At least, she could hope that the scandal would be *small*.

The two weeks in Bath revolved around Margaret Garnett's well-staged journeys to the Pump Room. But also, this visit was providing a perfect setting for Lady Jarman to assay the nature of the girl's deportment in society, a sort of introduction to London.

So far, thought Lady Jarman, she could ask for nothing better.

Corliss, however, held a different view of this alteration in her circumstances. Over her shoulder, as she and Isabel descended James Street, she said, "Your grandmother is a formidable personality, Isabel. I don't even yet know how it happened that I agreed to go along with this havey-cavey scheme. I can't imagine setting myself up as a London belle. I must have been mad!"

"Not mad, dear Merry—I mean, Corliss. I suppose I must learn to call you by that name now. How much more comfortable it would be to keep on calling you by your real name."

Corliss bit back the exclamation that nearly escaped her. It was certainly more than coincidence that Lady Jarman should pitch on her right name to be used as an alias! If Corliss were prone to see the hand of Providence at work, certainly this would be a prime example. Prosaically, she realized that, given that the book had fallen out of her lap to the floor open to the mention of the Hewett family, it was inevitable that Lady Jarman would select the name of Corliss Hewett as belonging to an old family without any pretensions to elegance and in fact—as Lady Jarman clearly considered—a family that had for the most part died out. But when Lady Jarman cried out, "Corliss Hewett! Just the right name!" Corliss's wits had completely left her.

"I wonder what our cousin Douglas is like," continued Isabel after a moment. "Near death, my grandmother said. I do hope," she added with a worried frown, "you get him to offer before he dies."

"What a dreadful thought!" said Corliss. "You are ghoulish!"

"Not at all, merely practical. If he does not sign my great-grandfather's unentailed estate over to us, well—I just can't think what will happen to us!"

"Who is the next heir?"

"I'm not sure, but I know it is not Geoffrey."

They left James Street and turned toward the center of town. For a little way, Isabel walked beside Corliss. "Do you really mind, Mer— I mean, Corliss? I know you don't like it *much*, but it's *our* whole future! And you don't have to marry the man, you know, and nurse him the rest of his life, even if it is short. All you have to do is—"

"I *know* what I have to do!" interrupted Corliss crossly. "I owe your mother a great deal, truly more than I can repay, but—I really cannot say I like it."

Isabel brought up a question that had not yet been asked of Corliss. "Where would you be if you were not here in Bath? I do not wish to pry, but we have wondered, where were you going on the stage, before you fell? You mentioned a position in Yorkshire? Do you think your employer will hold your place for you?"

"I doubt it." Mischief touched Corliss. "I cannot think this sort of scheme is quite the best training for a governess, can you?"

Isabel hesitated. "Governess? I thought you said companion, the other time."

So I did, thought Corliss. Again she thought, Not the first lie, but the second and the third. She would have to watch her tongue.

There was no one who cared about Corliss except these dear new friends the Garnetts. She could not bear it if she lost their esteem. And whatever she could do for them was little enough recompense for the great affection and tenderness they had all bestowed on her.

There was nothing she could say to the younger—by a mere three years!—girl looking so anxiously into her face.

"Did I offend you, dear Merry?"

"Of course not," said Corliss with a smile. "But, let us bury once and for all the name Meredith Havens, shall we?" She turned to walk on. "If we do not hurry, we shall not have time to spend at the bookstore. We must not be late for tea, or your mother will worry."

How nice to have someone to worry whether one were late even a few minutes—to say nothing of being six weeks overdue!

Corliss walked on in lighter spirits. The die was

cast, and she was—once again!—Corliss Hewett, but this time she had a purpose in her life, and she would do her best with it.

ii

The book shop drew Corliss like a magnet. She had been given, by her governess, the love of reading, and while she had not had the advantage of a regular course of study, she had taken advantage of her father's library.

Of course, she had not found any novels or other light reading in those dark leather-bound volumes on the shelves. But she had a good friend in the seamstress in the village, and that woman was more than willing to lend her own books, given to her by ladies of her custom who wished the books out of sight of husband or father, but were not willing to give up the source of titillation in their ordinary lives.

If ever I have more money than I have now, she thought, I must spend it on books. So, while she had no funds in hand, yet she considered herself as a potential customer, and entered the shop with assurance.

She was not aware that she had lost Isabel as she might have anticipated at the milliner's establishment next door to the book shop.

The lovely smell of books—the glue, the leather, even, she fancied, the ink—was a soul-satisfying aroma. She did not know how long she spent, browsing among the old and new books. An old favorite, *Lay of the Last Minstrel*, caught her eye. Holding the soft leather-bound volume in her hand, she was carried away in memory. Her dear governess and she had read this stirring poetry one summer day. She could almost smell the newly cut grass, hear the murmuring of bees in the rose garden . . .

She put that book back, but there were others. *Lyrical Ballads, Lady of the Lake*. She lost all sense of time. She was living in a queer frame of mind, where names changed and changed back, where everything she had known had been wiped away, where she was set down miles and miles from her Yorkshire destination. But just for a little while, here in the book shop, she could forget the currents that tugged at her.

A voice spoke almost in her ear, as one might imagine one's conscience might. "You are finding difficulty in making up your mind what books you wish to purchase?"

She looked up quickly, into the man's interested, kindly face. He was tanned, as though he had been much out in the sun, but there was an underlying pallor that, together with the cane on which he leaned, no doubt explained his presence in this city.

"Oh, it's not that I could not decide! It is only that I cannot take all of them."

"I quite agree with you. When I was much younger, I determined upon a blissful career operating a shop such as this. I believe, however, that I had the intention of opening the doors perhaps once weekly, and spending the rest of my time in a back room somewhere, reading my way through the shelves."

"Rather than a back room," Corliss smiled, entering into the spirit of the exchange, "I should prefer a window seat."

"With a piece of fruit?"

"And my cat!" she exclaimed, suddenly missing Miranda.

"It is probably a good thing that we do not find our wishes granted. If I had, I should likely be blind by now!"

Corliss thought, His features are certainly plain, and yet in some vague way they seem familiar to me. I am sure I have never met him, but a gentleman such as this was not ordinarily seen at Hewett Manor. His gray eyes, set above high cheekbones, held an amused twinkle. Most likely they could, however, turn into cold chips of granite if he grew angry.

Belatedly, Corliss realized she was speaking with too much cordiality to a man she had not met. But surely, a mutual interest in books ought to serve as an introduction? She herself might think so, but she was in no doubt as to what Lady Jarman would say.

Not quite knowing how to withdraw, she was relieved to see Isabel entering the shop. Where had she been? Corliss had thought she was near at hand all the time, as she should have been.

A tall gentleman of military bearing followed Isabel in, and there was a glint in his eye that indicated, even to Corliss, an unwonted interest in the girl. Such familiarity must be stopped at once.

She turned to her recent companion, whose converse she had much enjoyed. She was no better than Isabel! By now she had no doubt as to how to leave him. Politely, of course. "Good day," she said to him, not noticing the sudden chagrin on his face, and crossed the room to Isabel. "I think we must leave," she said, sufficiently loud to reach the ears of Isabel's admirer, and giving Isabel a speaking glance, she led the way out of the store.

"What did that man say to you?" she demanded of Isabel.

"He didn't speak. Corliss, I hope I know better than that! That is, he merely held the door open for me."

"Isabel, it was wrong to encourage him. Don't you see, he thought you were one of the lower orders." She walked a few steps before she added fretfully, "How distressing it is to be so deceitful! If we were here in our proper selves, how much better it would be."

"Soon we can be, if all works out as Grandmama plans," said Isabel practically.

"It is only that we must be careful. We cannot encourage handsome gentlemen of any kind, not until we have—finished what we came for," she ended lamely, shying away from saying the word *betrothal*. A word, she considered, far too final and even far too out of reach.

"When we do meet your cousin, he must not think I am a loose woman, or we will not get him up to the mark." Corliss was speaking to herself more than to Isabel.

"Of course, you are right," Isabel agreed good-naturedly, "but you must agree, he is so handsome!"

"Yes indeed, but you must remember you look like a servant to him. Not look like, precisely, but dressed like one, and if you are serious about playing that part when we get to London, then you must never let your guard down."

"Do you think—he might come to London? And he'd think . . ."

"Really," said Corliss in a confidential tone, "I have no idea whether he will come to London." Or the gentleman who was so pleasant behind the book rack, she added to herself. "But we have one purpose in mind in London, and I fear the slightest misstep will bring it all down in ruins."

"I'm sorry," said Isabel in a rush. "I keep forgetting—that's because you have the hard part. All I have to do is pretend to be the parlor maid, and I guess that will be difficult enough. Certainly, I must be more careful."

"It is in all probability I," said Corliss, gloomily but grammatically, "who will ruin all."

On this pessimistic note, she fell silent, and the girls returned to their rooms without further words. Each was lost in her own thoughts, and while the sense of them might have been put into words such as "What an appealing gentleman!" they would not have been speaking of the same man.

iii

Not far from Lady Jarman's rooms, near Queen Square, stood a tall, narrow building containing rooms to let. There, Captain Wheeler had found rooms for his colonel and himself. They had arrived late one recent afternoon by hired coach from Bristol, where their ship had docked after running into strong headwinds in the Channel. While the rooms looked in daylight rather dingier than they had the night before, Colonel Douglas Renfrew was too exhausted from his recent illness and the hardships of the journey to face a removal.

"Even the lumps in the mattress," he said the next day, "are English lumps, and therefore to my liking. Charles, I did not think I disliked Spain as much as I now believe. I even look forward in time to meeting a dainty miss with rose-petal fair skin and golden ringlets. Shall you be jealous?"

"I think not," grinned Charles, much encouraged by the continuing return of his dear friend from his extremely serious illness. "You recall, I take great care not to make acquaintance among the quality, lest I say something that leads to facing a parson."

"But you must marry sometime, Charles. And by the way, your expressed intentions do not in the least fool me. You'd like nothing better than to marry your rose-petal girl and retire to the country."

"All in good time, Douglas. Believe me, I shall approach my intended wife—whoever she is—from ambush. I've learned better than to stand in an open square and wait to be surrounded and brought down."

Douglas smiled. "You might consider revising your speech so that you don't make every encounter sound like a foray against the enemy. I imagine a delicately nurtured young lady might take exception to being regarded in the same light as a Norman castle. Do they not prefer romantic courtships? At least, so I have heard."

Charles burst into laughter. "I suppose you're right. But just now, that's the way I view 'em all—enemies of freedom. *My* freedom, that is!"

They had been in Bath for ten days—an excessively tedious ten days, at that—when Douglas Renfrew encountered Corliss Hewett in the book

shop. For all he had rallied his friend about looking for a lass with blond ringlets, he found the
dark-haired lady with eyes of a startling deep blue,
poring through volumes of poetry and speaking
about them with such assurance, very attractive
and beautiful.

He was, however, slightly relieved when she bade
him good-bye, for he saw, over her shoulder, his
good friend entering the shop in clear pursuit of a
humbly dressed girl possessed of the required
golden curls and fair skin. He was, further, somewhat dismayed to see that his new acquaintance, if
one could call her an acquaintance when he did
not even know her name, to say nothing of not
having been properly introduced, was the mistress
of Charles's most recent quarry.

Complications—he needed no more of those. So
he said nothing to Charles about his bookstore
lady, and listened with only half an ear to his
friend's raving about his discovery of the most
delicious porcelain-figured abigail in the millinery
shop.

Time to leave Bath, he was sure, on Charles's
account. But he himself wished heartily to see his
own discovery again, and if he were fortunate he
might even find someone to introduce them.

Soon the last day of his projected stay arrived,
and in the intervening time he had diligently attended the Assembly Rooms both in the morning
and the afternoon, hoping for a glimpse of her.
Not until he was about to give up the search
knowing that he must leave for London the next
morning, was his search rewarded, in a way. He
had just entered the room, stunned again by the
volume of sound that emanated from large num-

bers of well-bred men and women, when he caught
sight of her across the vast room.

He almost did not recognize her. She was wearing a bonnet in the abominable new fashion that
hid her features from the public, but then he
thought he would have recognized her graceful
walk wherever he might see it. He was, although
he did not know it, in the first stages of an attraction that, given his serious nature, was no fancy to
be gone in a day or two.

He strained to see whoever was accompanying
her, with the idea that someone must be found to
present him properly. He could not force his at-
tentions on her without that necessary introduction.

However, she was apparently alone. Mrs. Garnett and Lady Jarman were in another of the
public rooms, with Isabel the maid in attendance,
and Corliss, well on her way to complete *ennui*,
strolled aimlessly past palms and invalids in equal
numbers. She did not admit even to herself that
her boredom would vanish in an instant were she
to catch sight of that gentleman she had met once
before, in the book shop.

He had been in Bath for the waters, she was
sure, for he had been leaning rather heavily on a
cane. It was not beyond possibility that around a
corner she might come face to face with him again.
He was not in sight.

Since she was not expected to rejoin Lady Jarman
and her daughter for some little time yet, she
picked up from a nearby table an abandoned copy
of the *Gazette* and glanced idly through the various notices. Deaths—of no one she knew. She smiled
to herself, remembering that she had once wondered whether Cousin Elizabeth might have died

between the day she had written to Ralph about Corliss and the day Corliss's own note must have reached her.

That event would have explained everything to Corliss's satisfaction, but Lady Dacre's name did not appear among the deceased. However—

Her half-brother's name leaped from the page to her eyes.

She stared at the brief notice, giving merely the barest facts, but facts which stunned her.

"Sir Ralph Hewett has announced his recent marriage to Mrs. Theresa Ludlow, formerly of . . ."

Corliss's vision blurred. Frantically, she blinked back the tears lest she create a scene in public. She read the notice again. There could be no mistake. Lady Jarman had not found any other Hewett in England. It must be Ralph.

Somewhere within her, anger stirred, Ralph the poverty-stricken, who could not even keep Corliss in decent style. Ralph, who had shipped her away from her own home . . .

The reason was blatant. So he could marry this— this Mrs. Somebody—and he had never even mentioned the woman's name to her.

The letter, that was it. The letter he had been reading that day, the missive he had thrust into the desk drawer before he brought out Cousin Elizabeth's letter. And Corliss had had a chance to read it the day that she looked for her mother's brooch!

Her anger grew. By now she was shaking with fury. He had shoved her out, treated her like an unwanted pet. She supposed she was lucky he had not shot her, as one did a useless horse!

Well, this was the final crushing blow. She had

thought she no longer relied on him, but now she knew that at the back of her mind, and even tucked away in a corner of her heart, as it were, Ralph had existed as a last resort in case of disaster. Rather like a Norman keep, she thought, where there might be safety at the last.

Now the keep had fallen, and she was naked to the elements.

Except—some time later, she had calmed herself to remember *except*—she was not alone. She was an "adopted" Garnett, and she was cared about.

As though a curtain of some sort had been ripped away with the sudden shock of learning of Ralph's unheralded marriage, Corliss saw herself clearly. She had been playing a part until now, she had been toying with the idea of pursuing the Garnetts' colonel, because she had still held at the back of her mind the thought that she did have a bolt-hole.

Now—she *was* a Garnett, the colonel was a legitimate quarry of her "family," and she insensibly lined herself up totally without reservations on their side of the coming expedition.

A vagrant thought struck her. She hoped the colonel might be half as nice as the man she had met the other day at the bookstore.

She sprang to her feet and made her way into the next room in search of Lady Jarman and the others.

The colonel, striving to make his way through the throngs that filled the rooms, made little headway. He had watched the color drain from her face at something she had seen in the newspaper. After a moment, her cheeks had flushed and she had shortly risen and left the room. Even hurrying, stick in hand, he was not swift enough to keep her in sight. He had come so close, he thought, and yet had lost her. Even the newspaper was gone, so he had no clue to what information had caused her distress.

Regretfully, he went back to his rooms. He could not postpone any longer his business in London.

iv

Lady Jarman, suddenly impatient, harried her daughter and the entire household, setting them all in a turmoil to packing and preparing to remove to London.

"I have just heard the most disgusting news," she said, when pressed by her entire family to explain the sudden haste. "I know you are not quite yet the thing, Margaret, but there is no time to lose."

"What disgusting thing?"

"Why nobody told me in time to profit by the news, I cannot think. I shall know who my friends are—or at least are not—in future."

"Mother!" said Mrs. Garnett finally, and in a warning tone. "I shall suffer a relapse within the hour if you do not explain why we are all at sixes and sevens to get to London, when I doubt very much if the house is in order yet."

Thus brought to the point, Lady Jarman informed them, "I have just learned that Douglas Renfrew has been in Bath for more than a sennight, and *I did not know it!* And what's more, now he has left for London."

"So?" said Margaret Garnett. "Perhaps he is not as ill as your informant told you at the first."

"And perhaps he is," countered Lady Jarman. "At any rate, we could have brought dear Corliss to his attention, and now we would be at least halfway to a betrothal."

"Oh, no!" objected Corliss. "Not so soon!"

But then, she thought, why did that matter? Ralph was married, and without the slightest hint to her that he had matrimony in mind. At the back of her mind, and unexpressed except in an uneasy reluctance to hasten the courtship of a man she did not even know, was the thought that when the betrothal was announced and the Garnetts had their windfall safely in hand, what would become of Corliss Hewett?

"The sooner the better," said Lady Jarman grimly. "We must remember that he has been invalided home, and that means he may not have long to live."

"But suppose," said Isabel, "that his leaving Bath means he is recovering?"

"Then," insisted her grandmother, "all the more reason to get him in hand before every mama in town realizes that he and his fortune are ready to hand."

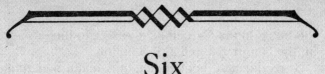

Six

i

Corliss, of necessity, had become something of a philosopher in recent weeks, although she would not have recognized that description as pertaining to herself. Having had so little of material benefit in her life, and having suffered a stunning series of shocking buffets of fate—or in other words, blows originating in her half-brother Ralph and her mother's cousin Lady Dacre—she was now of a mind to enjoy the only London Season she was apt to have.

She was well aware that only a limited sum of money was to be furnished by Lady Jarman in what Corliss was beginning to recognize as a desperate, last-chance throw of the dice, and therefore an expeditious progress toward the longed-for goal of a betrothal notice in the *Gazette*. Lady Jarman's household, both in Bath and in London, was scaled down to a bare minimum. There were no funds in the Garnett safe, either, to hire a staff in the country as well as in London.

Lady Jarman, besides her own maid, had sent for her cook, her butler Minch, and a groom and coachman. The Garnett family was called upon to provide a maid for Corliss and Mrs. Garnett, and a footman for duty in the foyer of the London house, as well as to run errands as they might be required. Thus it was that Isabel and Geoffrey found employment, unsuitable but in the long run, if all went well, enormously to their benefit.

"Just like charades," said Geoffrey stoutly. "Nothing to it." But a close observer might have noted that enthusiasm to match his words was lacking.

But Corliss was in London at last, and she determined to seize upon the joys of the capital with both hands, as it were. There was Lord Elgin's loot from Greece to see, a group of the most astonishing marble figures yet seen in England, and still not complete, for another and final shipment of marbles was expected to arrive next year. There were paintings in the Royal Gallery to admire, there were the famous treasures in the Tower of London—she was determined to see them all before disaster struck.

If disaster were to strike, that is. Lady Jarman would not admit the possibility of defeat, to say nothing of what Mrs. Garnett called disaster. All that money spent, she said more than once, and still we're sure of nothing.

"But dear Corliss is a bewitching young lady," pointed out Lady Jarman, "and anyone but a sworn priest must respond to her charm. We have counted on that from the start."

"But," objected Mrs. Garnett, "he has been *wounded*. And we don't really know, do we?"

"Wounded! Of course we know he has been wounded. What has that to say to anything?" scoffed Lady Jarman, but a small note of uneasiness could be detected in her voice.

Suddenly, the possibility her daughter was considering swept in on Lady Jarman like a spring tide. Suppose, just suppose, that his wounds, either the one that had brought him, so she believed, home to England or perhaps a previous wound, had rendered him—she phrased it delicately, even in her own mind—in a condition of *enforced* celibacy!

And Douglas, whom Lady Jarman remembered quite clearly from his early years, was a man of such integrity that he would not offer for a wife if he labored under such a disadvantage.

Ah well, she thought darkly, we'll wait and see. And if need be, I shall think up another ruse. Such as, perhaps, simply explaining the situation of the Garnetts to young Douglas. Margaret had already endeavored to enlist Mr. Ackley's good offices on her behalf, and been snubbed for her pains. However, Douglas himself had the final word, and if all else failed, she must approach him herself. She shrank from this last plan, because if Douglas, as might well be the case, had become hardened in Spain, if his character had been altered under the pressure of grim warfare and he had become greedy, there would be nothing more that could be done. Simply appealing to his better nature, when she did not know whether he still possessed one, was more of a gamble than even she was willing to take.

No, now all depended on the girl Merry—that is, Corliss, Lady Jarman corrected herself. To that end, Lady Jarman's plans moved ahead at a rapid pace.

Corliss was stunned at the variety of purchases that could be made. If one had unlimited funds, one could be decked out like a peacock—a very expensive peacock, to be sure. She became acquainted with the shops, although she bought little, and those items were purchased with Lady Jarman's sovereigns—Grafton House for muslins for morning gowns, Bedford House somewhere near Henrietta Street, and Newton's in Leicester Square. On Wigmore Street she found Flint & Clark. There were shoemakers and staymakers' shops, umbrella makers and fan makers.

Isabel and Geoffrey were required to accompany Corliss. At last Geoffrey rebelled. "Ribbons and furs and feathers—is there nothing else in London? I vow, Grandmama, I see no reason why London should be made much of."

Lady Jarman and her daughter had been busy on their own, leaving cards, calling, renewing ties with old acquaintances who were still in London. The Little Season was due to open in September, but Lady Jarman's plans took full notice of the advantages to be gained by ensnaring Douglas Renfrew before the great influx of young ladies and their mamas from the country.

But at length there came a breathing spell. Mrs. Garnett was becoming too fatigued to be useful. "I think I have been made ill by those dreadfully nauseating waters I took in Bath. If one wasn't ill to start with, I cannot think such pungent liquid could be beneficial."

Lady Jarman and her butler Minch had the plans for the first salvo—that is, the ball to introduce Corliss to London—well in hand. It was odd, thought Corliss, how often her mind turned to military images. Perhaps the reason lay in their constant recollection of Colonel Renfrew's recent army service and the wounds or illness that had brought him to England.

"You may as well see something of London," said Lady Jarman at breakfast, "as long as you are still not required to be on duty. Geoffrey, would you like to see the Tower? I am sure Augustus would like to see the animals. You may have the coach. And Sophie too will enjoy the outing."

The children, Sophie and Augustus, who spent much of their time in the schoolroom at the top of the house, were ecstatic. Poor Jerome was too young to be included, but the others, including Isabel and Geoffrey more or less in their own persons, swarmed down the stairs and into the coach without delay.

"Pray wear something very unassuming," said Lady Jarman to Corliss. "You will not wish to call notice to yourself in public before the ball next week."

Obediently, Corliss pulled from the back of the wardrobe the same gown she had worn when she took the stage at the village. It was clean now, of course, but if Lady Jarman wished simple garb, then this plain muslin filled the requirement.

The coach held the five without comfort. Corliss, Isabel, and Sophie occupied the forward-facing seat, and Geoffrey and Augustus sat opposite.

It was fitting, thought Corliss in amusement, that after noting all the thoughts of besieged castles, of military expeditions to capture the colonel, in a sense, that she would find herself playing the part of an ordinary tourist, visiting the most perfect medieval fortress in England. But she, no less than the younger Garnetts, fell under the spell of the ancient buildings. Even the White Tower, the keep of the first fort begun by William the Conquerer, still stood, looking ready if required to withstand Napoleon.

They saw the very place where Anne Boleyn had been executed, and the enormous giant's suit of armor and standing next to it, a small suit fit for a dwarf, or, as the custodian told them, Prince Henry, who died when but a lad. But at length their spirits flagged, overcome by so much sadness, the wretchedness of murdered queens and traitors seeming to linger in the very stones of the buildings. Corliss, especially, longed for the sight of the coach, and a nice dish of tea.

"What next?" she asked. "Shall we go home? My feet will not be fit to walk on by tomorrow! Sophie, what did you enjoy the most?"

Sophie, clearly developing ghoulish tastes, said promptly, "The place where the queen lost her head!"

Augustus's young voice shrilled, "What good is that? I liked the armor best. Why were they so small, Merry? I mean, Corliss? Why even Geoffrey could fit into some of that armor. Would you have gone on Crusade, Geoffrey? I mean, if we all were alive then? Would you go and leave Mama—and me? I would have been brave enough. I'm very brave, Corliss."

Without particularly noticing their direction, they had entered a narrow passage that seemed to lead toward the gate where they expected their coach to be waiting. There were a few other visitors also trending that way. What an enormous place this was, thought Corliss. It had to be to have accommodated a fighting army, the royal family, and even the government of England in perilous times.

Suddenly, Corliss, sniffing the air, knew they had taken a wrong turning. The smell reached her and Isabel at the same time. It was a feral smell, raising the hackles on the nape of the neck, an odor like all the stables of the world together, together with some frightening element added.

"The menagerie," said Isabel.

"Oh, let me see! Let us go, Corliss. Isabel . . ."

"We cannot disappoint Augustus," said Corliss.

"Especially now. I had thought he had quite forgotten about the animals."

He had not. Letting go of Corliss's hand, he broke into a run down the corridor ahead of them.

"Geoffrey, stop him!" cried Corliss.

"He'll be all right," said Geoffrey.

They all moved forward and caught up at last with Augustus. There were indeed animals somewhere very near, judging from the unpleasant smell. The visitors were in a kind of viewing gallery, from where they could look down into a semicircular paved area, shaped to fit the Lion Tower itself. Around the walls were arched openings, each containing a kind of two-story cage for the lions. The central area was open, and one supposed that the lions on their free days might gather and gambol together.

There was a strong sense of shadowy movement behind the grilled openings to the cages. The musky scent rose overpoweringly and Corliss felt burning at the back of her throat.

"Augustus, have you not seen enough?"

"Where are the lions? I don't see the lions."

Whether it was an instinctive response to the boy's shrill voice or not, Corliss did not know. But from the dimness below them came a growl, a kind of cough that sent shivers down her spine, and then—a roar of defiance that roused the echoes in the tower. The roar roused the other lions as well, and the reverberations rang back and forth until she thought they were inside her head.

When she recovered, she realized that Augustus was gone.

"Augustus . . . !"

As one, the group turned and ran back the way they had come, after Augustus. He had covered some distance before they reached him, and would doubtless have continued on his flight had he not run headlong into two gentlemen who, like themselves, were seeing the sights.

One of the men had a cane, and Corliss stopped short. "Did he hurt you? Augustus—"

"Pray do not scold the boy," said the man with the cane, and Corliss looked up to see her friend from the Bath book shop. "I should have taken to my heels as well."

Then he recognized Corliss, and they stared at each other in disbelief. Neither could find words, nor did they need them. As for Douglas, the sweet smile on his features told her everything she needed to know. On Corliss's part, she forgot the need for circumspection, even for decent veiling of her feelings, and the gladness that shone in her eyes would have warmed the heart of a marble statue. In truth, it quite undid Douglas Renfrew.

His companion touched his arm. With a strong effort, Douglas broke the spell that held Corliss and him, and, looking down at the boy, still clinging to his legs, said heartily, "Now then, young man, you're not afraid of a little noise, are you? If you look around, you will see that you are quite safe. It was only sound and fury, after all."

Augustus, turning to Corliss, said, "I am brave, truly I am. It was only for a moment that I forgot."

"Of course you are," said Corliss, hugging him. She handed him to Geoffrey, and, as though by chance, she found herself strolling back along the corridor toward the Bell Tower with the man she did not know was Douglas Renfrew.

He was delighted to see her again, he told her. He had found her in the Pump Room after looking for her for several days, but he could not reach her in time.

"You were reading a newspaper, and I fear something you noticed caused you distress."

"Oh, you were there then?"

"Too far away to be of service, I am sorry to say."

"Nothing could be done. Besides," she said with a mental shrug, "it's in the past now."

Douglas Renfrew had not in his younger years come to London to obtain what was called "town bronze," a term which in his mind equated with a passion for gambling and other means of wasting time and money. Instead, he had gone into his regiment directly from his university. While he was a considerate and well-mannered gentleman, he was impatient of the rules by which the *ton* lived, if indeed he was aware of them. All he knew now was that the young lady who attracted him was walking beside him, and he wished to become better acquainted with her.

On her part, Corliss knew the rules. There were things one did, and things one did not do, no matter how strong the inclination to continue strolling down the corridor with him might be. She knew that this was not a proper conversation to hold, nor, casting a glance toward Isabel and the other gentleman, could this chance meeting be encouraged. Indeed, she must extricate them both as quickly as possible from an uncomfortable situation.

She spoke hastily. "We must go at once. Isabel, Geoffrey . . ." She gathered the children around her, and said a polite farewell. She was not aware, however, that her dark blue eyes shone with a warmth that her cool voice could not deny.

He smiled at her. "Of course you must go. But now that I know you are in London, I shall find you, never fear."

"Oh!" she said. "You must not."

"Why ever not?"

"I cannot—I cannot tell you. But pray, do not try to find me. I am only a visitor in London, after all."

"But when," he persisted, "must you return to your home?"

"Home?" she echoed as though the word were new to her. "Quite soon, I think." She was babbling, she knew, and truth was not pertinent to the situation.

Later she did not remember how they reached the coach, or any details of the ride back to Lady Jarman's house in Hanover Square. She did remember the sudden shadow in the gray eyes. But she was pulled in two ways at once. This man and his obvious feeling for her—a feeling that she suspected she might gladly return—must be forgotten at once. She had an obligation to fulfill, and that duty did not include any man whose name was not Douglas Renfrew.

ii

The next few days saw Corliss moving in a sort of dreamlike state. Her new friend had told her, "I'll find you, never fear, now that I know you're in London." But she did not see quite how he might accomplish such a feat of detection. She had had her hands entirely full in those last few moments. Augustus, his mouth wide as Fingal's Cave, had not been silenced entirely until they reached the coach. Embarrassed by the child's bawling, both Corliss and Isabel devoted their efforts to calming him, feeling the eyes not only of the two gentlemen, but also of many other curious visitors to the Tower, following their progress toward their coach.

There had been no opportunity, had either of the girls wished, to exchange names. She recalled that Geoffrey, obviously misliking the entire incident of meeting the strange gentlemen and finding one of them too familiar with Corliss, and embarrassed to his bones by the unseemly behavior of his brother, had taken Sophie by the arm and jerked her along in the wake of the rest of his hurrying family.

Later, when Augustus's tears had been wiped
away and they had returned to Hanover Square,
the entire episode glossed over, Isabel turned
thoughtful. She knew she had seen the gentleman
before, in Bath with Corliss, but there was something about him, as seen in the dim corridor leading to the Lion Tower, that puzzled her. Somewhere, she believed, she had seen him even before
the Bath encounter. But where on earth could she
have? The only other time she had been to London was weeks ago when she and her mother had
come up to see Mr. Ackley, in vain, and of course
she had never been in Bath except for last week.

She was not given long to brood upon the answer to the puzzle. In truth, soon she began to
believe there was no puzzle at all, but only a cob-
webby figment of her imagination. Besides, there
was far too much to do to allow her to engage in
futile memory-chasing.

The ball was upon them. It was a small affair, as
balls go, and did not even include a sit-down dinner beforehand. Lady Jarman declared she per-
sonally abominated the usual dinner fare in London, and she would not inflict it upon her friends,
to say nothing of Douglas Renfrew. She had sent
out his invitation card first of all of them and his
acceptance was received promptly, as was only
proper in the case of a family connection, as he
was.

"I can recall many a dinner that would today
send me to my bed for a sennight. Potatoes, tur-
key, sausage, pickles, all kinds of vegetables—and
the wines! I vow that after sherry or hock with
every course, one was hard put to balance half a
dozen different morsels on one's fork."

"At the same time?" Sophie demanded to know.
"Of course. It was quite the fashion. But we must consider dear Douglas. Even though I am informed that he is restored to tolerable health, I should not wish him to be taken off by a stomach fever, at least until he has offered for Corliss!"

The hour for the ball finally arrived. Corliss was dressed in a shimmering white gown. She had refused the loan of Mrs. Garnett's pearls, preferring to wear as her only jewel her mother's pin, the opal surrounded by garnets. Violins played in an anteroom as the guests arrived. Soon Minch assisted by Geoffrey, passed refreshments, threading their paths through the throng, most of whom were just back from the summer in the country, and were anxious to greet their friends with as much enthusiasm as if they had just returned from Captain Cook's voyage to the antipodean continent.

Isabel, pert in her parlor-maid uniform, took from the arriving ladies wraps of such elegance as she had never dreamed of. An abundance of gauzy shawls, silver-spangled peau de soie, and one short cloak of swan's-down, so light it fairly floated into her hands. The ladies moved in a rainbow of glinting lights as the wax candles caught their jewels and reflected blue and green and red sparkles.

Although she could not fairly blame them, the ladies looked quite through her, and never at her. A fine disguise, she realized, so that when I come out in society in two years, no one will ever know they have seen me before. As the evening wore on, a constant stream of guests came through the door. Before long, Isabel found the aura of pow-

der and scent, in which the ladies moved as though
in a cloud, strong enough at times to catch in her
throat. She much preferred the sweet country air
to which she was accustomed.

And the chatter! Since they did not see her
except as a mere adjunct to the furnishings, they
spoke before her with unbridled tongue.

"I cannot believe that Lady Jarman wishes to
come into society again. And this Hewett woman,
who is she?"

"I've inquired, my dear, and she comes from an
old, old family that everyone thought had died
out. Probably without a sovereign to her name,
and after a rich husband. But I wonder what Lady
Jarman gets out of this sponsorship. She's not one
to do anything without advantage to herself!"

The first speaker, a woman with shining black
hair dressed in a classic chignon that suited her
langorous beauty, spoke again, and there was no
question as to her sincerity. "She had best not try
to cut me out. I have my eye on . . ." Her voice
dropped so that Isabel, though she held her breath
to aid her hearing, could not discover the name.
"And I shall allow no interference, I promise you."

Isabel did not think the whispered name sounded
like Renfrew. Lady Jarman must be correct in her
belief that few people knew Douglas was home
from the wars. His return from the Peninsula was
apparently unheralded, probably in light of the
fact that he was coming back as an invalid of sorts.
But Isabel, after the first rush of guests had gone
up the stairs to greet Lady Jarman and Corliss,
and before the next influx, had time to think, and
her thoughts were dark indeed.

Truly, if this were all that London society could

offer—a malicious propensity to unkind gossip, a hothouse atmosphere of scents and elegant clothes whose uses were decorative rather than useful, and perhaps a journey now and then to one of the sights of the town, like the Lion Tower where Augustus had been frightened out of his wits— then Isabel doubted that she longed for her introduction to society as much as she had previously done.

Was it all for this—for Isabel's matrimonial benefit—that dear Merry had been persuaded, reluctantly, to take on another name and present herself as bait for Colonel Renfrew? Isabel did not recognize the source of some of her new doubts, but an observer might have remarked that since Isabel had herself pretended to be a servant, although not oppressed, she had learned how much work was required to keep ladies such as those who had just now ascended the stairs to greet Lady Jarman in good looks and good spirits.

Good spirits! Mocking and full of ill will, rather!

And then she was jolted out of her pessimistic thoughts by a sight she had not expected. Geoffrey the footman, to use the term with which she teased her brother, opened the front door and ushered in the man from the Lion Tower, the man from the Bath bookstore, the gentleman who was so irritatingly familiar to her and yet whom she knew she had never seen before. The man's face, in the light of the wax-candle chandelier, still bore the dark touch of the sun she had noted before, although he had apparently abandoned his cane now. He looked straight at her and smiled at her, very kindly, apparently recognizing her from their recent encounter at the Tower.

And then she knew who he was—and whom he reminded her of, so that she thought she knew him.

He bore a striking resemblance to the portrait of Great-grandfather, the source of the evil will, an oil painting now kept hidden on a dark wall in the Garnett library. The paint had darkened over the years, and the painting had not been cleaned since she could remember, so it was no wonder that Merry had not recognized this man who admired her so.

Colonel Douglas Renfrew, the end and aim of this entire adventure in London, stood in Lady Jarman's foyer, already interested, to say the least, in M— Corliss! It is odd, thought Isabel, that I am not as happy as I should be.

Then, behind Colonel Renfrew, she saw the other gentleman from Bath, the man who had waited for her outside the milliner's when Corliss was in the book shop—the man who had smiled at her then, with a light in his eyes that assured her she was quite perfect and hinted that he was more than halfway in love with her already. The man from whom she had been forcibly snatched away by Corliss, in that encounter just outside the Lion Tower!

He was not lost to her forever! Now, she thought, now I am happy.

She could do no more than curtsy in her best manner. Geoffrey was watching her with a frown, so she supposed she must be doing something wrong. But her thoughts tumbled out of control, and she could not think. Then the moment was gone, and she watched their backs, tailored in the smoothest way by a master tailor, as the men started up the stairs.

Her brother strode across the hall to her. "What's the matter, Isabel?" demanded Geoffrey in an undertone. "You look daft!"

Of necessity, her wits returned, and she swiftly improvised an answer. "Didn't you see that man? The first one? It was Colonel Renfrew! He came, and you can see he's not near dying at all!"

"I knew that," scoffed her brother, "as soon as Grandmama heard that he had left Bath for London. But how do you know? He didn't wear his name on his forehead, did he?"

"Near enough," she retorted. "Didn't you see how much he looked like Great-grandfather's portrait in the library?"

"Never paid any attention to it," said Geoffrey.

"Young sir," came Minch's voice, "there's people coming. If you weren't who you are, and me bound to make exception, I'd see you out the back door without waiting till tomorrow!"

The butler sighed as though harassed beyond his endurance by the need to put up with his mistress's whims. Imagine, a son of the house playing at footman! And taking the bread out of some young lad's mouth! A young lad, moreover, whom Minch could bully to his heart's content. Minch gave less attention to Isabel's play-acting, for women were all alike and who knew what would take their fancy next! But young Mr. Garnett! Belatedly, he remembered his own place and spoke again to Geoffrey.

"Sir," he said, quite properly.

Isabel's surprise at recognizing Cousin Douglas, and her doubtless insufficiently hidden delight at seeing again the man who had taken her fancy in Bath, was as nothing to the shock that Corliss sustained when standing at Lady Jarman's right hand and greeting face after face with little expectation of remembering the names that accompanied them, she looked up to see features she knew. He was smiling, his kind smile that seemed as familiar to her as though she had always known him. His bright gray eyes rested on her with apparent delight.

Lady Jarman was speaking to him. "Douglas, I did think that you might have called on me before now. After all, we are quite nearly connected, and I have not seen you since before you left for that dreadful war. I did hear you were sadly wounded. Can that be true? You look most fit!"

Her voice trailed away as she realized she had lost her audience. Colonel Renfrew was engrossed in a rapt gaze at dear Corliss, a gaze that seemed to be returned in full.

"Corliss, my dear," she said, trying to regain control of the situation, "this—*this* is Colonel Renfrew. Margaret's husband's cousin, Douglas Renfrew." She emphasized each word, and at last was gratified to see that Corliss had remembered her manners.

"Of course," said Corliss, her lips saying words of civility but her eyes conveying an entirely different idea. "I am delighted to see you recovered from your wound."

"Not a wound, as Lady Jarman believes," he said, "but an irritating ague that would not leave me. But indeed, thank you, I am well on my way to restored health."

The gentleman behind Douglas was introduced

as Captain Charles Wheeler, and his sole asset as far as Lady Jarman was concerned lay in his discreet pressure on Douglas's arm to move him forward. Lady Jarman's thought took a new and not entirely welcome direction. It was clear to her—and most likely to everyone else in the room—that Douglas and Corliss had previously met. No one fell into such a passion for another at first sight!

iii

The next day, Lady Jarman pronounced the ball a huge success. "Corliss, my dear—how easily I remember to call you by that name, you see? —you did very nicely. I vow that all of London is lost in admiration of you. Besides, remembering our purpose here in London, one might almost think that you and Douglas Renfrew were on the verge of an understanding."

There was a question in her voice, but Corliss did not know how to answer it. She was in too much confusion herself to attempt to clarify the situation for Lady Jarman.

Corliss had been unable to sleep. She had sustained a shock when Colonel Renfrew was presented to her. She had not known quite what to expect, but it was certainly not *this!* From the first, she had not allowed herself to imagine what the colonel would be like. Indeed, she had been forced to bury the thought of the stranger to whom she must become betrothed.

More particularly and recently, because of her

liking for the new acquaintance she had made in Bath, she had stifled speculation at its birth. Her new acquaintance had been a gentleman of quality, of course, and when she met him again with the Garnett children at the Tower, she knew she liked him above half. But she could not allow herself to dream about this gentleman either, for first she had to fulfill her agreement with the Garnetts. Hurt deeply by Ralph's betrayal and the monumental indifference of her mother's cousin, she had no one to cling to save the Garnetts.

She had spared a thought to what might happen were her new friend to become interested in her seriously and she must give her attention to the unknown Colonel Renfrew—would her new friend remove himself from her life? Could she possibly explain to him the issue at stake?

Moreover, she had added to herself, in explaining to him, how would she justify the entire deceitful ploy? She could not! If only she could come to a resolution on this particular question, she would be happy, she had thought.

Now, faced with the reality that her new friend and her quarry were one and the same—the kindly gentleman with the slightly haunted look in his bright eyes—her dilemma was a thousandfold worse.

As these thoughts, not for the first time since last evening, raced through her mind, Lady Jarman continued to speak. When Corliss paid heed again, the older woman was saying, "He will of course pay a duty call on us this morning. Corliss, I wish you will wear that ashes-of-roses muslin. It sets off your dark hair so well."

She was torn in two by her guilty conscience

and what was becoming an urgent need to see him again. Now that she knew who he was, she also knew that she would see him often, as they moved in the same circles in society.

"I—I have the headache . . ." she began. Lady Jarman bent a quelling look on her, and she subsided. She must, of course, be ready to receive him. That was the point of the entire recent four weeks.

Whereas she had thrown herself wholeheartedly into the scheme upon reading of Ralph's surprising marriage, now she hated the necessity of keeping on.

"Very well," she heard herself saying. "I'll go upstairs and change at once."

Douglas made his duty call, and if it were less a duty than a heartfelt need to see Corliss again, he did not confide this fact to anyone. Especially did he not confide in Charles Wheeler. Charles was his nearest friend, his aide, and, in accordance with the wishes of the Iron Duke, his companion in his convalescence. But there were times when Charles grated on his nerves.

Charles and his pursuit of willing wenches, Charles and his determination to enjoy himself thoroughly before settling down on his northern estates—Charles could not be expected to understand the turmoil within Douglas's hitherto untouched feelings. For years he had been a soldier, and a good one. He had not dallied with the ladies of the Peninsula, for his mind was filled with his duties and, he told himself, he was too phlegmatic to fall prey to passion.

Since he had expressed himself on this subject

more than once to the more adventurous Charles, he did not see any need to inform his friend that perhaps he had been mistaken.

At any rate, today he had left Charles behind at their rooms, nursing a headache brought on by vinous indiscretion the night before. As he climbed the steps to Lady Jarman's house, he was less interested in doing his duty to his hostess of the night before than he was in catching a glimpse of the young lady whom—if she had not entirely captured his heart—at least he would like to know better.

Geoffrey the footman opened the door to him. Douglas felt a faint sense of familiarity at the sight of him. Was it only because he had been on duty here the night before? Or had he seen the lad somewhere else, in a different setting? Douglas shrugged mentally. He was becoming fanciful in the extreme. A belated effect of the fever, no doubt.

In the salon, where Lady Jarman waited to receive him, he suddenly became tongue-tied in the presence of Corliss, a vision in a gown the color of ashes of roses. It was a good thing, he thought, that he had not brought Charles with him. Charles was a handsome gentleman with great address, and—Douglas wondered suddenly if he were jealous. No, it could not be, for he had never been jealous in his life. But still, he was relieved that he had had the foresight to come alone.

Lady Jarman, surveying the two people in her drawing room, thought she had never seen as tongue-tied a pair. One might excuse a rustic swain twirling his cap before a pretty maid, but these two . . .

Ah, well, it all boded well for her aim in getting young Douglas betrothed, her daughter's family moved into comfortable circumstances, and herself free to indulge whatever whim she might develop. But for the first time, she began to wonder what she had wrought. Were Meredith—that is, Corliss—to succumb to the colonel's charm, what then? Would Lady Jarman herself relish the idea of a nobody wed to a Renfrew? Surely the girl would not pretend forever to be Corliss Hewett!

Corliss did not know, afterward, what she had said to Colonel Renfrew. She was still shocked by last night's discovery that the man she had taken such a liking to was indeed the man she was supposed to ensnare. How this would all come out in the end, she had no idea. But, as had happened so often in recent weeks, the only answer that came to her was no answer at all. She must simply drift on the current of events, and let what would happen, happen.

What was next to happen, she realized, was that she would view the Elgin marbles with the colonel. "I have been away from England for such a long time that I have not seen any of the changes in the city that have occurred," he explained. "I should appreciate your guidance."

With Lady Jarman's approval, it was decided that the excursion would take place the next day. "With her abigail, of course."

"Of course," said Douglas, as though he were not surprised. He had been away, he realized, from the niceties of decorum for too long.

"Isabel must of course go with you," Lady Jarmin told Corliss when they were alone. "It is most important that convention not be outraged in this affair, for we cannot take a chance on the colonel's feeling he has compromised you and therefore has to insist upon marriage."

"Marriage?" said Corliss, her eyes shining.

"My dear child, *you forget.* He must be led—and I shall see to that, never fear—only to the point of an official betrothal, and no farther."

The sparkle in Corliss's eyes died away. "Of course, Lady Jarman. I had almost forgot."

Later, alone in her room upstairs, Corliss reflected. I once wished that the colonel might be as nice as the stranger in Bath, and now he is. I mean, they're the same. And I think he likes me, at least a little.

She stared out over the rooftops of the neighboring houses, seeing only the colonel and her own dilemma. Suddenly her attention was caught by a familiar figure on the next street leading away from the square. It was Isabel, in her dark shawl!

The girl was walking demurely away from the square. Where was she going? Corliss suddenly realized that while Isabel was taking small steps as befitted a humble maid, yet she was covering ground at a good rate of speed.

At the edge of Corliss's view, the girl stopped. The other window in Corliss's room would provide a wider vista.

It did, indeed. Isabel was engrossed in conversation with a man of stocky but military bearing, a conversation that seemed to go on longer than might be necessary to answer a request for directions, for instance.

In a moment, Corliss recognized Isabel's gentleman. He was that captain who attended the colonel!

Suddenly, Corliss pulled back from the window. She had no business to spy on Isabel. Nor should she inform Isabel's mother of what she had discovered. In truth, she had discovered nothing, really. It was only happenstance that she had thought of the captain as "Isabel's gentleman." And yet, she could not deny that there could be a kernel of truth in the matter. Isabel's posture was surely not that of a humble maid responding to a casual question from a stranger. Far from it!

Seven

i

Corliss's ball had been attended by most of the quality then resident in London, and the sudden attraction between her and the mysterious Colonel Renfrew, who was new to London, had not gone unnoticed. Many a lady immured in the country, by desire or circumstances, kept up with rumors, gossip, and fact—not always distinguishable—pertaining to London society by correspondence from those garrulous ladies on the spot. Elizabeth Dacre was one of those country-bound ladies. She had returned from Scarborough to find that her young cousin had not arrived. Days went by, stretching into weeks, and there was no word either from Corliss herself or from the girl's doltish half-brother Ralph.

Lady Dacre's indolence, nurtured over a number of years of easy living and the assiduous service of her staff, prevented her from feeling any alarm. It was less trouble to believe that the girl had failed to measure up to her own standards.

Towne took full advantage of the situation as she saw it. "Too bad young miss didn't send word of some kind, if she changed her mind. And how a well-brought up young lady might change her mind on a journey in her own coach with maid and coachman and outriders, I cannot see."

She peeked quickly from the corner of her eye at her mistress to gauge the effect of her words. The frown on Lady Dacre's smooth brow was a satisfactory sign. Towne continued. "It's all of a piece, my lady, expecting you to take on a stranger without so much as a by-your-leave, and then changing her mind and never letting you hear. I call it abominable!"

Towne, for all her knowledge of her mistress, was not overly perceptive. Black and white she knew, but interesting shades of gray passed her by entirely.

"I cannot think . . ." began Lady Dacre slowly, speaking more to herself than carrying on a conversation with her maid, "I can*not* think that dear Fanny could have brought up a girl to be so unfeeling."

"But Lady Hewett's been gone this long time! Who knows what could have happened after she died?"

"Not that long ago, Towne. Three years, perhaps four. I do lose track. If the girl is, as I recall, twenty years old, then she will have had her mother until she was seventeen."

Towne picked up her mistress's morning's attire and gave it a shake, as though it were the young miss herself. Towne had no illusions. If the girl came to live with Lady Dacre, then she, Towne, would not only have more work to do after she had spent years in the successful effort to remove duties from her own shoulders to someone else's, but worse, it was possible, if the girl were smart enough or if the girl's abigail had her wits about her, that Miss Hewett would soon winkle her way into Lady Dacre's heart, and most likely into her will, a document by which Towne expected to profit handsomely.

"I misdoubt that something may have happened to her," fretted Lady Dacre, "and I should have inquired myself instead of waiting for Corliss to write. Suppose she is in trouble somewhere?"

Towne muttered, "Not likely," but Lady Dacre, engrossed in her own thoughts, did not heed her.

Lady Dacre did not take the opportunity to write the kindly letter she had intended to Corliss at Hewett Manor, or to Ralph, inquiring about the girl. In her private coach, she would be safe, she believed. And the coach must have been returned to Ralph, or he would have written to request the return of his vehicle and his servants.

The mail, however, brought an answer of sorts to her worries about her young cousin. Philomena Darrell, a widow with more money than sense, found her excitement in her voluminous correspondence.

"Dear, dear Elizabeth," she wrote, "this is such a dull Season. I vow I do not know why I stay in London in the summer."

Lady Dacre read with the mildest of interest until she arrived at the seventh page. "I must tell you the oddest thing. The other day Lady Jarman returned to town. You recall her, I am sure, the woman with the big teeth and the notion that she knows best for everyone. At any rate, she has opened her house for the first time in three years, and is sponsoring a young lady in society. A nice enough girl, I suppose, but Ly J has her hands full, I don't doubt. A mysterious colonel, very handsome and I am told quite rich, just home from the wars with some kind of fever, and the young lady at first sight for all we know could not take their eyes from each other. I have seen them several times around town, and they seem most comfortable together. I should imagine they will make a match of it. I looked up the Hewetts— aren't they connected with the Monteiths in some way? The girl has an odd name, Corliss, I believe. Corliss Hewett . . ."

Whatever else Philomena had to say went unheeded. Her letter dropped to Lady Dacre's lap and slid from there to the floor, while she sat stunned with the realization of what she could in the light of Philomena's news only consider Corliss's treachery. How dared the girl get her, Lady Dacre, excited with anticipation of her arrival and then, in some very odd way, turn up as a belle in the Little Season in London? Ralph's plea that he had not sufficient funds to launch the girl in her proper place in society rang false as a cracked church bell! How dared he! And for that matter, how dared Corliss?

It took the entire day and half the night before Lady Dacre felt her thoughts to be coherent enough to set words on paper. She had not Corliss's address in London, but she knew Ralph's direction well enough, and it was to him that she wrote.

"I have learned that your sister is moving in high circles in London, when I had expected her arrival here at Dacre Hall momentarily. I cannot believe that you would not have written me of your change of plans, and can only think . . ."

She paused as a new and alarming thought came to her. Corliss was not the only female, as it happened, who devoured the romances of Maria Edgeworth and certain other writers.

"The girl's been kidnapped!" thought Lady Dacre. "She must be a pawn in the hands of some villains! I know it!"

Even the recollection that Lady Jarman was an entirely respectable woman did not substantially alter Elizabeth Dacre's fearful conclusion. There was a mystery at the bottom of this very odd development, and she must probe to the bottom. No matter what she found, she thought dramatically. Her carefully cultivated indolence was fast disappearing down the wind.

She finished her letter to Ralph. "Fearing that something untoward is happening to dear Corliss, I must tell you that I shall open my town house and travel at once to London to look into Corliss's situation. Since you have not seen fit to inform me of your own altered plans for Corliss, I shall not trouble you with my findings. I only trust that I may not uncover a scandal of major dimensions. Believe me, etc., etc."

She gave detailed instructions to her butler, and then sent for Towne. "I shall not have time to have new gowns made for London," she told her maid, "so you will have to put what I have in good shape, and quickly. London will have to see me as an unfashionable country lady, and I care not. I must find out what has happened to Corliss."

Towne left her presence without a word. Downstairs, however, the cook and the parlor maid as well as a very new footman received a tongue-lashing for various faults that had little basis in fact and, as well, little effect on the recipients.

Indeed, all cook said was, "Miss Towne's nose is out of joint, that's what it is. Mind you, jealousy's been the downfall of more than one! If Towne isn't careful, she's heading right for a fall!"

ii

Ralph Hewett and his new lady had no such obliging correspondents in London. However, the missive from Yorkshire proved sufficiently inflammatory to set Hewett Manor in an uproar.

"The girl's in London?" echoed Theresa Ludlow Hewett, unbelieving. "You said you sent her to this cousin. How did she get to London then?"

Ralph winced at the shrill tone of his wife's voice. He was beginning to believe that the money to restore the Hewett estates would be hard won.

"How do I know how she got to London? Maybe it isn't my sister. Maybe someone just—"

"Just what?" Lady Hewett demanded. "Nobody would pick out a name like Corliss Hewett—certainly the oddest name anyone ever heard—and hope to get away with an imposture. Wouldn't they know that you would see to punishing them, or her? Besides, how would she find someone to sponsor her? If it is your sister."

Ralph, to give him credit, wanted to do the right thing. It was often difficult for him, since so many arguments pulled him in different ways. But now his duty was clear. If Corliss were not with Lady Dacre—as seemed evident from that lady's letter—then she must be someplace else. Not in London, for Ralph's imagination could not soar high enough to envision a fairy godmother of sufficient power to accomplish such an alteration in Corliss's affairs. He knew well enough that a ball in London meant a sponsor of quality and an adequate wardrobe, both entailing substantial expense. And Corliss had no more than half a dozen sovereigns in her hand, he was sure.

Havey-cavey wasn't the word for it. He must go to London himself to see this Corliss Hewett. He could only believe in an impostor.

"The nerve of that girl, running off like that!"

"You don't know what happened," objected Ralph.

"I know well enough. You promised me she would be out of the house. You said she'd gone to her cousin in Yorkshire. Well, it's clear enough to me. You've bungled the whole thing!"

Ralph lapsed into silence. There were some insistent proddings from his conscience, reminding him that he had been excessively shabby in his arrangements to send Corliss away. Lady Dacre's letter had hinted strongly that his coach and servants should have been sufficient to protect his young half-sister. He dared not admit even to

Theresa that Corliss had been put on an ordinary stage. He was surely to blame if anything had happened to Corliss.

Now he knew that he must make his own way to London to straighten the matter out. Belatedly, he considered the significant expense this would entail, and sighed, but to his credit he did not waver in his resolve.

Phyllida, Theresa's daughter, upon hearing that Ralph was going to London, insisted upon going along.

"You'll be of no good there," protested Ralph. "I will take your mother, but not you."

Recognizing a quality in her husband's voice that she had not heard before, Theresa agreed. "You'll have your turn, my dear, in due time." She rose to follow him upstairs to begin packing.

Phyllida reached for another biscuit, and proceeded to pile it high with damson plum preserves.

iii

"I wonder you are content to stay so long in London," said Corliss, strolling with the colonel in Green Park. "There is so little social life, and Lady Jarman tells me that we will not see a gay whirl of parties and dinners until September."

The day was fine, not too warm for August, and the park was in its best looks. If a spectator were at first surprised to note a lady and a gentleman of quality moving together along one of the walks, he would have noted Convention dogging their heels in the persons of abigail Isabel and footman Geoffrey. Lady Jarman, totally misreading the colonel, was certain he would be put off by the slightest breath of impropriety.

She would have been amazed, not to say stunned, to hear the colonel's expression of opinion.

"I would much rather not contemplate gay parties in September, or any other month, Miss Hewett. I do not doubt that there will be many suitors clamoring for the next quadrille, or whatever the fashionable dance may be. As it is now," he continued smiling, "I have your entire attention, save for that pair of servants behind us, and all of London's hundreds of thousands around us."

Corliss glanced at him from the corner of her eye. "But you too would find many ladies to charm you."

"I cannot agree."

They walked on a few moments in silence. Corliss had found that the colonel's company was immensely pleasant. Indeed, she had sprung awake more than once in the middle of the night in the grip of the certainty that she would have to manage without his company some day, and perhaps soon.

"I have wondered, you know, just how it is that you know Lady Jarman? Even Mrs. Garnett, who married my cousin, is a stranger to me, and yet you are not connected with the family?"

"Not at all." She must be careful not to tell him everything that had happened, for surely, if she were not to marry him, her affairs could be of no interest to him. There was the slightest spark in her thoughts that might kindle into a flame of

some substance, a spark that said, "You might not
have to cry off after the betrothal. You might
even marry him!"

She dared not think about such an eventuality,
especially when he was looking down at her, that
smile that could melt her just hovering at the
corners of his lips.

"We met in the country," she said, purposely
vague. "I hurt my ankle, and Mrs. Garnett was so
kind to me. I am certain your life must be much
more interesting. Have you been in the army long?"
She stopped short in distress. "Must you go back
to the war?"

"Would you care? No, no, that is not a proper
question to ask. Pray forgive me. I have been away
from England too long. I am no better than a
rough crude soldier, and if I am too forward, too
open in my speech, pray forgive me."

I will forgive you anything, she thought. "I am
not missish, to be sure," she said after a moment,
"but—"

"I understand," he said quickly. "I make you
uncomfortable. Very well, let us talk of other things.
I suspect that you had a lonely childhood like my
own. I was an only child, you know, and I found
my playfellows in the library. Fortunately, my mother's family catered to their scholarly inclinations,
and there was no lack of books to read."

"You told me once," she said shyly, "that you
had wanted to own a bookstore!"

"You remember that?"

"But you are such a man of action," she protested. "You could not have had time for reading
in Spain. I do not understand how it is in the

army, you understand, but I cannot think you could ignore someone shooting at you."

"Army life! I thought I would miss it greatly. You know, my men took the place of the brothers I did not have, and there was excitement and action, along with many days when we simply marched in the heat and the dust to get to somewhere else, no different from the place we left."

Othello could not have found Desdemona a more interested listener. The time slipped by, and the sun reached its zenith and passed it.

Corliss knew that upon reaching home she would be interrogated by Lady Jarman about what he had said, and what she had said, with a view to assessing the progress of the all-important courtship. She looked back on the conversation, and chose certain remarks that she would relate as the pertinent speeches of the day. She would tell Lady Jarman that the colonel had suggested that he escort her and perhaps Mrs. Garnett to the lecture series to start in the autumn in the rooms of the Philosophical Society in Fleet Street. Mr. Samuel T. Coleridge was to inform his listeners on the subject of the principles of poetry, using as illustrations both Shakespeare and John Milton.

Lady Jarman would pounce on the invitation, and Corliss could almost hear her expected comment. "We'll be done with London long before that, Corliss. You must bring him up to the mark before September, for to be quite frank, I am unwilling to commit additional funds. I shall tell you what to say to him the next time you see him. Shall I ask him to dinner, I wonder? A quiet family dinner? Perhaps that would be best."

Corliss shrank from the thought of Lady Jarman's

harrying of the colonel, like a fox chivvied by hounds. Imagine, feeling protective of an officer who had led his men, hundreds, even thousands of them for all she knew, into battle! He could surely fend off Lady Jarman!

However, there were things said that day, and other things hinted, that she would cherish in her heart long after Colonel Renfrew might have vanished from her life. Lady Jarman would never hear of them.

Corliss and Douglas turned at the end of the walk and started back in the direction of Hanover Square. "I cannot but admire," Douglas told her, "the way you pay such sweet attention to the children. The small boy frightened by the lions. I was quite envious. Have I distressed you again?"

"No," she said in a small voice. "But you see, it is very easy to be kind to children."

Douglas was taken back to a child in a Spanish village, buffeted by his father, kicked into bawling submission, one arm hanging limply. "Not always," he said.

Douglas realized that he was fairly in the grip of a passion he had never believed himself capable of. How had this sweet-faced, merry girl with the astonishingly dark blue eyes gained such a hold on his thoughts, even on his ambition?

He was scarcely aware that he was speaking aloud. "I think it is most of all your transparent honesty, Miss Hewett. One cannot envision any circumstance whatever that you would not deal with totally with truth. It is such a refreshing and rare quality in a lady—at least in the ladies I have been acquainted with. I prize it above all things."

Engrossed in his thoughts, he did not notice the

effect his musings had on his companion. *Honesty!*
If that were the quality he prized, she faced disaster wrecking the secret hopes she had tried not to
entertain. The small spark that might have flared
up into happiness was quenched as thoroughly as
though he had dropped a bucket of water on it.

He offered her his arm as they crossed the
street. She let her hand rest on his forearm for a
little longer than was required, and he took en-
couragement from the small act.

"I think that Lady Jarman must stand in the
position of head of your family? Shall you object
very much if I were to call on her in the near
future?"

"Call on her?"

Douglas put his ambition at risk. "You must be
aware of my feelings for you. I rather hope that
you may not be indifferent to me. I should like to
speak to you myself, but I believe it is customary
to ask permission of one who has you in her
charge."

It had come! He was about to offer, and he
would see Lady Jarman tomorrow, and by next
week all would be arranged.

She did have a choice. She could accept his
offer, and then cry off after the legal business was
done. Or she could snatch at her own happiness,
after all these weeks of thinking herself abandoned, cast off by Ralph, ignored by her cousin in
Yorkshire. She could keep her secret, trusting in
the Garnetts—two of the family now following
discreetly behind her—to protect her disguise, and
marry him.

And then sometime in the future, when she had
all but forgotten the rather sordid reason for her

meeting him in the first place, it might by chance all come out, and she would be undone.

Deceit in itself was a lesser sin than keeping the secret hidden for months, even years. And the man beside her now, the man she knew she loved above all other humans, would be revolted by her dishonesty, and thus her happiness would be destroyed.

"You are very quiet, Miss Hewett," he said gravely. "Is my company then so distasteful to you?"

"No, Colonel Renfrew. I—have things to think about, that is all."

She consoled herself by saying, there is no deceit truthfully, for I *am* Corliss Hewett. I am not in London under a name not rightfully mine. But she knew that if Lady Jarman and Mrs. Garnett were to explain the events from their knowledge, beginning with her climbing into the coach at the first, no one would believe she was who she was. Ralph might be invited to vouch for her genuineness, but she did not know him any more. The brother who was capable of sending her off in shabby fashion and directly thereafter marrying someone she had never heard of could quite easily decide to have nothing more to do with her. And, as a last desperate gamble, there would be no hope left if Ralph denied her.

"I shall be greatly pleased," said Douglas rather humbly, "if your thoughts include me."

This she could answer honestly. "Oh yes, they do!"

The leaping joy in his eyes told her what convention had bade him keep silent. She knew, now, that he did love her. That love she could not lose.

She would keep her secret to herself, and trust to Providence, which had done quite well for her so far.

They walked back to the Hanover Square house in a roseate dream, not shared in the least by the bored brother and sister attending them, some distance in the rear.

Eight

i

During the next fortnight, Corliss and Douglas moved in a kind of euphoric rosiness that gave rise to envy in Charles Wheeler, the satisfaction of approaching triumph in Lady Jarman, and a foreboding of doom to come in her daughter.

"There's no doubt that she'll get him up to the mark. I give her another week, and then it is time, if he hasn't spoken, for me to suggest very strongly to Douglas that he must declare himself," boasted Lady Jarman. "I think you must admit, Margaret, that all our trouble has been worth the while? And I do think that Isabel has well earned her Season when she is eighteen, for she has not complained a whit about playing parlor maid."

"And Geoffrey too," maintained Mrs. Garnett, springing to the defense of her eldest son. "He is the dearest boy."

"Of course," said Lady Jarman. "In fact, I think

he has been more devoted to duty than Isabel. There are times when I cannot think where she could be!"

After a small silence, Mrs. Garnett, still not strong after her drastic cure at Bath of the nonexistent illness that had taken them there, said in a worried tone, "Mama, I cannot like it."

Lady Jarman bristled. "What don't you like about my scheme? I think I did very well for you. That legacy is as good as in your hands right now."

"But he's so much nicer than I thought he was. You know, Mr. Ackley gave me the grimmest picture of the man. Now I think we should have waited until Douglas came home, and then just asked him."

Lady Jarman sniffed. "I have never known a man to give up income rightfully his, just because some relative asked him for it. No, no, Margaret, this way it will be done all legally, and no questions asked."

Margaret Garnett shook her head slightly. Although she would not argue further with her mother, yet her mind was unchanged. She did not like the arrangement.

"I wish we had not had to ask Isabel to play parlor maid," said Mrs. Garnett. "When I bring her to London in a couple of years, people may remember her."

"Nonsense. In two years, most of these women in town will not remember their own sisters if they have not seen them in the interval." Lady Jarman thought a moment. "I do say, though, that she is nobody's idea of the perfect servant. A good thing she will not have to earn her living in that way. She is altogether too saucy."

Mrs. Garnett pleated her skirt between nervous fingers. "Mama," she said on a note of desperation, "do you like that Captain Wheeler that comes here with Douglas?"

Lady Jarman stared at her daughter. "What do you mean, Margaret? Why should I even think of the man?"

"It seems to me that I have seen him look at Isabel in such a way. I do hope—"

"Nonsense! Surely the man would not seduce my parlor maid in my own house." Certain incidents now occurred to her, however, sometimes no more than a fleeting glance, that took on a new significance. More thoughtfully, she added, "but I must admit that the girl is far less biddable than I expected. Margaret, she must take after the Garnett side of the family. I would think she was a direct descendant of that perky actress that old Renfrew married, the one that made all the trouble about the will, except that she had no children."

"I shall have to speak to her," said Margaret, without enthusiasm.

"Ah, well, a word of warning ought to be sufficient. Captain Wheeler is obviously not planning to marry a servant, and if Isabel remembers her present position in the household, all will be well."

Lady Jarman, now in a confidential mood, continued. "I don't deny that I did have doubts at the start. Not about Isabel, but Meredith herself. There were no living relatives, according to that county history, but someone somewhere must have known some of the family. I half expected an indignant dowager to ride up and tell us that Corliss Hewett was dead and buried, and who was this wench!" She laughed at her own fancy, and Margaret managed a reluctant smile.

"At least that hasn't happened," agreed her daughter, "but—I hope we can get to the end of this without disaster."

"What disaster?" demanded her mother. "Nothing can go wrong now!"

They were interrupted in their cozy conversation by the butler, wearing a mystified expression. He stood in the doorway, and announced, "Lady Dacre, my lady." He swallowed, and added, in a voice suitable for calling attention to the Apocalypse, "Miss Hewett's cousin."

Lady Dacre entered the salon to see the two occupants of the room half standing as though pulled up by an unseen force from their chairs, and staring at her.

"Good morning," said Lady Dacre with cool dignity. "I should like to see my cousin, Corliss Hewett. I am told she lives here?"

"No, she doesn't!" exclaimed Margaret.

"Yes," said Lady Jarman simultaneously, "she does."

Lady Dacre lifted an eyebrow. "May I see her, please?"

Mrs. Garnett abandoned the arena. Lady Jarman, aware of the excruciating curiosity behind Minch's protruding eyes, told him, "That will do," and waited until the door was closed firmly behind him before she spoke again. "Lady Dacre, I believe you said? I fear we have not previously met. And you claim to be Corliss's cousin? We did not know our dear girl had any relatives."

"She has. And I do not merely *claim* to be her cousin."

The best defense, thought Lady Jarman, near to panic, is an active offense. She managed an insolent tone. "We would certainly have left it to you, then, Lady—Dacre, is it?—to bring her out into society. The girl is twenty years old, after all, and we could not believe that her relations—if they existed, that is—would not have her best interests in mind. She is the dearest girl, you know. You must regret deeply that you have come too late."

Having successfully, so she thought, put Lady Dacre in the wrong, Lady Jarman allowed a small smile to touch her lips.

But Lady Dacre was no novice in the cut and thrust of conversation. "The girl was on her way to me in Yorkshire," said Lady Dacre sturdily, "when she fell into your hands—or perhaps you would prefer the word *disappeared*? At any rate, I must take exception to the fact that you did not see fit to inform me of my cousin's whereabouts."

"Oh!" said Mrs. Garnett. "But she wrote to—"

Lady Jarman sent a quelling glance toward her daughter, but it was too late.

Lady Dacre smiled and sat back in her chair. "I will admit that at first I was most indignant, fearing my cousin to have fallen into the hands of villains. How often one's first impressions are correct, are they not?"

"Why should you suspect villainy when you knew nothing of what had happened?"

"Villains, without a doubt," repeated Lady Dacre. "No respectable persons would overpower a young girl and cause a coach and four and several servants to disappear, would they?"

"But that's not the way it was!" cried Mrs. Garnett.

"Never mind, Margaret."

"But that *must* be the way it was. Unless—I cannot have been mistaken, surely? If you are truly Lady Jarman, and not an impostor—no, no, I cannot see it. Perhaps you will be kind enough to send for Corliss now? I shall not rest, I assure you, until I have seen her myself."

Lady Jarman recognized the true distress driving the other woman. But the lady must be disabused of her misconceptions, for the young lady in Lady Jarman's present care was not Corliss Hewett, and the sooner Lady Dacre realized that, the sooner she might find the cousin she searched for. But what of Corliss—her Corliss—and Douglas Renfrew?

"But we are respectable, Lady Dacre. Surely you must realize we are not what you think?"

"It is possible that you may convince me of that fact. However, I am waiting to hear your explanation of events. Then, I shall wish to see my cousin and hear what she has to tell me before I decide on my next step."

Towne would have been stunned to hear the note of firmness and decision in her mistress's voice. Even though Lady Dacre's life had run along smooth lines for the past thirty years, she had not altered in essence. She had in her young years known how to deal with inferiors and miscreants. A part of her mind now smiled upon her and told her she had not lost her touch.

She listened carefully for the next fifteen minutes to a confused explanation voiced antiphonally by Margaret Garnett and Lady Jarman. Toward the end, a frown touched her forehead.

"Then you do not know Corliss Hewett?" she asked doubtfully.

"Not at all. It was mere happenstance that that name was chosen."

"How did that happen? Did the girl suggest it?"

"No," said Lady Jarman. "I myself did. She was reading a book, a county history, and it dropped to the floor. I picked it up and chose the name from its pages. I did not think there would be any relatives. The family seems to have died out entirely."

"So your protégé then is not Corliss, but she must have a name."

"She is Meredith Havens. A young girl who slipped and sprained her ankle getting down from the coach. A public stagecoach, you know, not a private carriage at all. That is all I can tell you. She wrote a note as soon as she realized she could go no further on the stage. But no one saw to whom it was directed."

Lady Dacre seemed to have shrunk in size. Not only was there no villain, but Corliss herself seemed lost to her. She could not quite approve of the motive for the imposture, even though Lady Jarman put it in the best light possible, but that was of no significance now. Corliss, her coach, her servants, all were as though wiped out of existence. She did not know where to look next. But look she must, until she knew what had happened to the girl.

At last, stiffly, she rose from her chair. "I must trouble you no further," she said, "but if you do hear anything, will you let me know? I live in Portland Place."

Lady Jarman was tempted to take her elbow and assist her, for she looked very fragile, but she refrained lest she insult the woman.

Lady Dacre had got as far as the foyer when Geoffrey the footman opened to door to two people entering out of the sunlight. Here, Lady Dacre knew, was the girl called Corliss accompanied by a gentleman. She put out her hand to stop the girl, and looked earnestly into her face, almost as though she were memorizing her features.

"My dear," she said in a shaky voice, but very kindly, "I am so sorry."

Whether she was sorry for the girl or for herself could not be determined. Towne emerged from the coach where she had been told to wait, and helped her mistress down the steps. The interview had not gone well, she was pleased to notice, and expected to hear the details later.

When Lady Dacre was settled in her coach and the vehicle moved smoothly away, she put her hands up to cover her face. "Too bad," she said, her voice muffled, "but there was something . . ."

In the meantime, Corliss, accompanied by Douglas, greeted Mrs. Garnett and Lady Jarman. "Who was that lady?" asked Corliss. "Should I know her?"

"Not at all," said Lady Jarman briskly. "She introduced herself as Lady Dacre."

"L-lady—" Corliss's voice rose sharply and broke off, as she slid through Douglas's arms onto the floor in a dead faint.

ii

Corliss, soon recovered from her faint, still kept to her room. She had many things to sort out in her mind, and without delay. She had quite liked the looks of the woman who she was told was Lady Dacre, Cousin Elizabeth. But it was quite clear from the manner in which she had looked at her that she had not recognized Corliss at all.

Nor was there a reason why she should, since she had not seen her before.

But there was one thing that she had not thought would rise up to demand her attention. It was clear, from Cousin Elizabeth's arrival in London and her coming to inquire after Corliss, that she had indeed taken note of Corliss's nonarrival. She must have received her note, perhaps belatedly, and then taken steps to find her.

How unsettling it was to find out that Cousin Elizabeth did care what happened to her! She was not alone in the world, then. How she wished she had known that before.

Before she had become so enmeshed in her feelings for Douglas Renfrew that she could not imagine a future without him. She had not lied, truly, for she *was* Corliss Hewett. But the scheme that the Garnetts and Lady Jarman had induced her to undertake tarnished her in her own eyes. How much darker would the stain be, then, to Douglas?

This afternoon, strolling through Green Park with him, was quite the happiest she had ever known. She knew he was far from indifferent to her. "One thing that I admire greatly about you," he said, "is your affection for your family. It is such a genuine emotion, too, for I know you well enough, I believe, to be sure you are incapable of pretense."

That would have been sufficient to bring her to

tears, had she had time to think about the dark deceit that moved her, but he went on. "I cannot imagine," he said with the directness of a soldier, "anything worse than to have a—a person close to one whose word one could not rely on."

He had been on the verge of saying, "a *wife*," she was positive. And all she had had to say would have been Yes. But the opportunity now was lost forever. Even if he did not learn of the scheme to ensnare him, she, Corliss, knew about it. She could not carry on with the plot.

But the Garnetts depended on her . . .

A tap on the door roused her, and with some relief at the interruption to her own uncomfortable thoughts, she called out to enter. Lady Jarman opened the door and came in.

"My dear, I must apologize for—well, quite frankly, I do not know quite what to apologize for, but there must have been something that occurred in the foyer to upset you. Do you know Lady Dacre?"

"No, ma'am, I do not. At least, I have never seen her, but I do know who she is."

When Corliss did not continue, Lady Jarman prodded, "And just who is she, besides a lady of quality from Yorkshire? Oh, yes, I made some inquiries. Don't remain silent, Meredith. If there is something we need to know, I think you must tell us."

Corliss squared her shoulders. "Yes," she said at last, "I think I must."

She sat in a chair opposite Lady Jarman, her unfocused gaze concentrated in the direction of the hearth, and told a straightforward story. She did not see Lady Jarman's wincing reaction to the journey on the stage, to the note that was written and somehow did not reach Lady Dacre. But when it came to the decision to call her Corliss Hewett, Lady Jarman could no longer contain her surprise.

"Your own name? Truly? Meredith, I cannot believe this. How could such a coincidence happen? I myself chose it out of a book. You had nothing to do with it!"

"I've thought about that," said Corliss. "At first I thought that it was the hand of Providence showing me that I should go along with the scheme, even though I am unused to—deceit."

She stopped short. Her claim sounded wildly inappropriate, since she had gone to the Garnetts as Meredith Havens. She hurried on, hoping that Lady Jarman would not notice. Her hope was vain.

"Why did you call yourself another name at the start?"

There was nothing for it but to be honest, a resolution that was coming, at best, a bit tardily. "Because—that is, because I did not know Mrs. Garnett. And I did not want my family, my brother Ralph and Cousin Elizabeth, to be ashamed of me, traveling on a public stage, and forced to ask for help from strangers."

"When you are alone, whom else would you ask but strangers?"

"It was an impulse." Corliss rose and began to pace the room again. "A mad, stupid mistake."

"But why," persisted Lady Jarman, "why did I fix upon the name Corliss?"

"Because I was reading the county history," said Corliss, much disturbed, "to see whether I had any relatives, even remote ones, besides my cousin that I could write to. Cousin Elizabeth had not answered my letter, and who else was there?"

Lady Jarman had a quick vision of Corliss leaping to her feet, the book sliding from her lap to the floor, and lying open—to the Hewett family. She had made this same explanation as a sop to Lady Dacre, but now she knew she had told only the truth.

"Perhaps," she murmured, "your first thought might be correct. The hand of Providence, indeed. It has brought you here, at any rate. And, my dear, I do believe that your cousin did not receive that letter, for certainly in her indignation at learning there was an impostor in London, she did not mention hearing from you."

"Then she believes I am an imposter?"

"Pray sit down, Corliss. That pacing gives me the headache. I certainly received the impression that she did not know you when she saw you in the foyer. But perhaps that is understandable, if you have never met."

Corliss, as bidden, sat down. "What can I do? I cannot go on, Lady Jarman. I have lied to so many people—"

"Not 'so many people.' Only our family, and we are equally guilty, if there is blame to be apportioned. But I have eyes in my head, and it is clear to me that no one matters to you but Douglas Renfrew."

Unable to speak, Corliss put her hands up to cover her face and nodded miserably.

"I do believe that Douglas is strongly attracted to you. He will likely forgive you for anything."

"Not for dishonesty. Not for deceiving him."

"There is time," said Lady Jarman, clinging to

what she feared was a lost hope, "enough to tell him. And after all, what is there to tell? That you are not related to us? He knows that."

"But I cannot marry him without explaining all this."

"My dear," said Lady Jarman, a firm note creeping into her voice, "you are not required to marry him. Only bring him up to the mark. That's all you must do. You may cry off as soon as the betrothal is in the *Gazette*. Time then for explanations, if you feel you must."

Corliss's only response was a renewal of heart-catching sobs. Lady Jarman rose to leave. Looking with kindness on the girl's bent head, she placed a comforting hand on her heaving shoulders. "He may not want to let you go, you know. And you could do worse than marry him."

"Never!" cried Corliss, her voice thick with tears. "I will not marry him under false pretenses, and he will never forgive me, I know."

Curious, Lady Jarman inquired, "False pretenses? I do not understand you, Corliss. I suppose your name will come more easily to my tongue now. But I do not see wherein you have deceived him. By the greatest good fortune, the name we chose for you in this little ploy happens to be your own. Where is the deceit?"

Slowly, Corliss agreed. "I suppose that is so. But the entire plan was to set a trap for him—"

Lady Jarman was suddenly amused. "You keep speaking of marriage. Has he offered without talking to me? I had thought him better-mannered." She looked at Corliss with a good deal of affection. "Well, I must go and tell the family all about our dear Corliss. I think we will all be well advised to adhere strictly to truth in the future. After, of course, we have the famous betrothal well in hand. It would be ineligible to let all this work go to waste. And a certain expenditure of funds, too. Now we must see what we can do," she said, relenting. "By the way, about your brother. Are we to expect his arrival momentarily?"

Corliss explained about Ralph, and the shocking news she had read in the journal at Bath. "And he never said a word about his marriage. I certainly do not expect him to come to town looking for me. He has all but disinherited me!"

One odd thing about that was that she did not care. Another odd thing was that she was entirely wrong.

At that very moment in the Hewett coach, traveling rapidly toward London, Corliss was the object of a rancorous conversation.

"If your sister had any sense about her," said Lady Hewett, "she would be making up to Lady Dacre. She's a wealthy woman, is she not?"

"I suppose so," said Ralph sullenly.

"I imagine so, for she spoke in her letter about opening up her London house. Imagine, having a town house ready for you whenever you chose to say, Open the house. But I don't understand. Why did your sister not write to you to tell you she was in London? How is it that you must get your news from some relation? Why is your sister in London in the first place? You told me she was going to Yorkshire."

"I thought she was. It ought to be obvious to anybody," he said waspishly, "that something has gone wrong. I was too optimistic, I see, to send

her out alone, but I had to." He looked signifi-
cantly at his bride.

"You're not going to blame me for what you
did, Ralph. I had nothing to do with your sending
your sister away."

She had already forgotten her ultimatum to him,
thought Ralph, but it would serve no purpose to
remind her. He had learned in these few but
seemingly interminable weeks that no argument
was ever won until she had said the last word.

"Besides," said his lady with an air of satisfaction, "we must support Lady Dacre in her search
for your sister. I am sure she could do much to
our advantage, were she to take a liking to us.
And think of Phyllida! Only three years before we
shall bring her to London. How fine it would be
to have Lady Dacre sponsor her!"

Ralph closed his eyes and appeared to sleep.
His mind, however, was as active as it had ever
been behind those concealing eyelids.

They had taken rooms at Pulteney's Hotel, and
he looked forward to a room whose furniture
stayed where it should and the floor did not move
up and down to the rhythm of the trotting horses.
He could not believe that Corliss was in London,
coming into society under the wing of a certain
Lady Jarman, with whose name he was unfamiliar. How could she have gotten to London? How
did she meet a titled lady in the first place? Surely
people of the quality of Lady Jarman did not
travel on the public stage?

Nor should, his conscience told him belatedly,
his sister have gone north in such a havey-cavey
way.

Guilt, automatically revealing itself as anger, was

a strong force in driving him to London. If it were
his sister, she had an explanation to make to him,
and it had best be a good one. If the Corliss
Hewett in London were an imposter, well—he
hoped he would know how to deal with that!

His intention was to go to this Lady Jarman's
house, demand to see his sister, and, after reading
the riot act, make some disposal of the girl. Newgate
if she were an impostor—Hewett Manor if she
were truly Corliss. He looked forward with even
less enthusiasm than previously to the thought of
two women, who disliked each other as he was
positive they would, bickering in his household.
But first, he must see Lady Dacre. Perhaps she
had already found out the truth.

He did not know he had spoken aloud, until
Theresa agreed with him. "Oh, yes, we must win
her favor, no matter how."

Nine

i

By the time Sir Ralph and Lady Hewett had
arrived at the hotel and been installed in their
rooms, he had altered his first decision. He had a
dreadful vision, born of his wife's clearly spoken
intention to ingratiate herself with Lady Dacre, of
Theresa's vulgarity coming out—perhaps not in
words or even deeds, but a fawning way of obvious toadying that would result in the most morti-
fying experience of his life. He would not take his
bride to Lady Dacre and expose Theresa to certain
setdown in a way that only the quality could do.

He was not sure whether his reluctance lay in
his concern for Theresa or for himself.

"I will go alone," he told Theresa, "to this Lady
Jarman's house. I have learned she lives in Hanover Square—"

"Hanover square? That is not quite as elegant as
Lady Dacre's address, is it?"

". . . and see this girl," he continued as though his wife had not spoken, "that calls herself Corliss." Even though he spoke as if he expected the girl to be an impostor, yet he was certain he would see the real Corliss. But whether she were there on her own or not, whether she had been drugged and brought to London for someone's nefarious purposes, he would deal with the situation as it arose.

He presented himself at Lady Jarman's town house at a most inappropriate moment. He could not, of course, have foreseen that his arrival would coincide with a family conclave in the large salon. From behind the closed doors he could hear a momentarily raised voice that he did not recognize.

Minch, resenting any interruption to his eaves-dropping, opened the door to him and allowed him to enter.

"I came to see Miss Hewett," Ralph told the butler. "Pray fetch her to me."

Minch placed a slight but perceptible distance between himself and the rude visitor. "I fear the family is not receiving this afternoon. Sir."

"I did not ask for the family. Be good enough to inform Miss Hewett that I am here. And you may say also that I intend to see her before I leave."

Minch abruptly relinquished his responsibility. "What name shall I say, sir?"

"Ralph Hewett." He eyed the butler narrowly. "I suppose you've heard my name before, eh? I'm not overlong on patience, so suppose you inform my sister of my arrival at once. And I want to see her alone."

In case, he added to himself, she is being held

prisoner. He could not believe that she had come to London, ignoring Lady Dacre, forgetting what was due to Ralph himself, except under some form of coercion.

Opening the door to the salon allowed a burst of anguished sound to reach Ralph, even though he could see no part of the room. At that moment, Corliss, on her feet, was crying, "I don't know what to do! But I'll not lie any more!"

Unfortunately, these words, in his sister's voice, came to her brother like a trumpet summons to battle. Suddenly indignant, he followed on the butler's heels into the salon.

The scene was not what he expected. In the first place, it was an elegant room. No lack of money to take care of the furniture here! And the persons in the room seemed to be disposed in amiable and even domestic fashion around the room. A young man, his back to the company, stood looking out of the window at the far side of the room. Lady Jarman, as he supposed, was seated regally in a high-backed chair, clearly presiding over the company. A younger woman, with light brown hair, sat arrested, startled by his arrival.

And Corliss.

She stared at him, stunned. "Good God, it's Ralph!"

"I thought you underestimated your brother," said Lady Jarman. "I am much relieved to see that he really is your brother. He certainly recognizes you, as he would not Meredith Havens. Or whoever. So you really are Corliss Hewett. I confess the story was a little too novelish for me to accept wholeheartedly."

Corliss swung toward her. "You still thought I lied? But you said—"

Lady Jarman, a charming hostess under any circumstances, rose and advanced toward Ralph. "I believe you must be Sir Ralph Hewett? Our dear Corliss's brother." Then, with incredible aplomb, she added outrageously, "And what brings you to town?"

Ralph could not quite ignore his hostess, but he did his best. "Corliss, what is the meaning of this? Lady Jarman, I must ask to see my sister alone. I do not wish her to be influenced unduly by—"

"By whom?" interrupted Lady Jarman smoothly. "I collect that your solicitude for her has not to this date been overwhelming, or you would have known where she was. And, considering that you sent her off alone on a public stage, I believe you cannot be as surprised at her present state as you try to persuade me."

"Corliss!" said Ralph sharply. "Where can we talk, privately?"

"Ralph," said Corliss, her color high and her breath coming in short gasps, "I do not wish to talk to you privately." She pulled herself up, seeming to grow taller before his eyes. "Anything you have to say to me you can say before these people." Greatly daring, and hurt much more deeply than she had thought by his secret marriage, she added, "My new family, Ralph."

"What are you doing here?"

"I am enjoying myself. Why did you come?"

"To get you out of the hands of these villains!"

"Nonsense, Ralph." Corliss was becoming easier in her mind. She had had great shocks in recent weeks, not the least being the belief that her brother did not care for her in the least, but this confrontation with him seemed to clear her mind of a number of doubts on a good many questions. "You come a little late if you thought I was going to be ruined. We have been in London for three weeks already."

No one, not even Minch, realized that the street door still stood open. The scandalous and unheard of accusations flying back and forth like arrows from crossbows claimed his unfaltering attention. He was of two minds, and could not at the moment decide whether he would give his notice on the spot, or whether to linger, await the most interesting outcome, and then give his opinion that no butler of decent habits could accept such goings on.

However muddled the butler's wits at the moment, the tense drama he watched unfolding in the salon had totally captured his interest. No one noticed the approach up the steps, and into the foyer, of Colonel Renfrew. The colonel was, in truth, screwing his courage to the sticking point and rehearsing in his mind certain words to be addressed to Corliss, upon which he would attain his heart's desire, her promise to marry him.

Douglas, not knowing that Corliss was struggling desperately in the clutches of a bad conscience, had been for some days puzzled at her waywardness. For the most part, their companionship had been idyllic, euphoric, totally satisfactory.

But at times, for no reason he knew, she would turn cool, even troubled. If he were the cause of her sometimes aloofness, if she did not truly like him, then he must know.

When he had, occasionally, spoken about addressing Lady Jarman on a subject important to them both, he saw that Corliss, at least recently, had not greeted the suggestion with anything approaching enthusiasm.

He must know—he needed to know what troubled her, and if it were his presence, or his intentions, then he must—

He did not know what he must do then. But he could not live in this state of uncertainty much longer.

Preoccupied as he was, the colonel was not immediately aware of the tenseness emanating from the salon, around the bulky figure of Minch standing in the doorway. But when he did become aware of his surroundings, he stood rooted to the spot. The angry words he overheard appalled him. Clearly, he had arrived at an inopportune time.

"How did I know you weren't in Yorkshire?" shouted an unfamiliar masculine voice. "There's something very suspicious about this entire affair, Corliss. What's the purpose? If it's to get money out of me, you've not a chance."

Lady Jarman interposed, "But we have not asked you for money, Sir Ralph. And I should like a little more decorum in my salon."

"Decorum, is it? It's my belief you haven't the slightest idea of what is owed to my family."

"Please stop, Ralph!" cried Corliss. Douglas suspected that she was near to tears, but from anger or from some other emotion, he could not discern.

"I owe you nothing, and you know it."

"You've only a short while before you're of age, and your own mistress. No matter whose you are now!" Douglas's fists clenched and he breathed heavily through his nose. "In the meantime—"

"In the meantime, Ralph, you may stop insulting me. Go back home and shout at your new wife!"

"Jealous, Corliss? I had not thought of it of you. It's these new friends of yours, these partners in some scheme I do not understand. But I'll tell you, Corliss—you are none of *my* family!"

It was at this point that Douglas Renfrew retreated. Rarely in his life had he been forced to withdraw in temporary defeat from an untenable position, but he found that at this point too many unknown factors had emerged for him to advance. Withdrawal was indicated—and subsequent regrouping before he forged ahead again.

It was also at this moment that the young man in footman's livery but clearly not on duty, standing by the window, stared with sudden intensity at something or someone on the walk who had caught his eye. He turned to speak, but saw that no one in the room was in the least likely to listen to him, so he remained silent, but thoughtful.

Lady Jarman moved to interrupt the stormy dialogue between Corliss and her brother, but Corliss forestalled her. Moving to stand directly in front of him, she said in an altered tone, "Ralph, please just go away. I know what I'm doing, and no one forced me to it." As well hang, she thought, for a sheep as a goat, and added, mendaciously, "I'm totally contented here, and believe me, I don't regret a moment with the Garnetts and Lady Jarman. Please, Ralph, don't you see you're spoiling everything?"

Offended, Ralph sniffed. "I came all this way to see whether you were all right, Corliss. I'm not

sure that you are, but I see there's nothing I can
do about it. Just remember, I wash my hands of
you and you can go to the—to the devil, for all I
care!"

Suddenly feeling as though she were back in the
schoolroom, where her older half-brother often
dropped in to pick a quarrel, she said now, in
childish but honest anger, "You too!"

ii

Geoffrey, knowing that he had seen something
from the window that no one else had seen, was in
a dilemma.

He knew full well the extent of the scheme to
ensnare the colonel. The reward for success would
be significant, and after all, as soon as the colonel
got himself betrothed, to any woman whatever,
that idiotic will devised by his great-grandfather
would operate, and the unentailed estate and a
more than adequate income would come to the
Garnetts.

But Grandmother had to leap to conclusions,
and concoct a scheme that had not the slightest
chance of succeeding, he could see now. Geoffrey
forgot that he had been as enthusiastic as anyone
when the scheme was first put into play. He was
even willing at the start to let Minch harry him—at
least as much as the man dared—to cut down the
cost of the two months Grandmother thought it
would take to get cousin Douglas into the toils.

The trouble was, he thought morosely, first that

Grandmother was wrong and the man was not next to sticking his spoon in the wall. The second thing was that he was entirely disgusted with bowing and scraping in front of the colonel, who knew nothing of who he was, and favored him fleetingly with a kindly smile. And the third thing was that he quite liked the colonel and did not quite approve of the way the women of his family had made common cause and hunted the man down like a fox ahead of the hounds. This fox, though, seemed more than willing to join at least one of his hunters.

That is, until this very afternoon. Geoffrey had seen from his window vantage point, not the arrival, for he had been looking mistrustfully at Sir Ralph at that moment, but certainly the departure of the colonel himself.

The colonel had obviously overheard all that went on in the salon, for the door was open, and Geoffrey would not have been surprised to be told that the upraised and belligerent voices had carried to the end of the street.

Besides, now that there was so much stir about a missing letter, he remembered that he had seen that very letter in the inn at the crossroads, and had said nothing to anyone. Guilt lay on him. There was only one thing to do, and Geoffrey proceeded to do it. He went up the stairs and sought counsel of Isabel.

"I don't understand, Bel. Is Corliss really Corliss? That's daft. How could Grandmama pick out her real name?"

"I don't know."

"Then Corliss isn't going to try to get the colonel to marry her?" He spoke as one anxious to nail down all the questionable points in his mind.

Thoughtfully, Isabel said, "I cannot see that will make any difference. He's so attracted to her. Grandmama thinks that nothing will put him off now." She sighed, enjoying her first near view of great passion. "He won't know she's deceived him, because who will tell him? Not us! And once the offer's made, we'll be rich!"

"Not rich. But it will feel good," said Geoffrey morosely, "to have a real footman for a change. I can't say I take to the position. But what do you mean, no one will tell him?"

"Only Sir Ralph knows that Corliss is—well, Corliss! And he washed his hands of her. I don't see that it will make any difference anyway. After all, she's not going to marry him."

"Do you like the idea that Corliss has done all this for us? What is she to gain out of all this? No money, certainly, for it is to come to us. And not a husband, either. That family of hers, if her brother is a sample, is worse than useless. All she gets is the satisfaction of seeing us with a better income, and what good is that? And what happens to her afterward?"

Isabel, dropped abruptly to solid earth out of her rosy romantic dream, stared at him. "I hadn't thought of that. I've been so busy trying to remember to curtsy and not speak out of turn—"

"And," interrupted her all-seeing brother, "trying to catch the eye of that captain friend of Colonel Renfrew's. I'm beginning to wonder, Bel, where you disappear to every afternoon. I suppose that Captain Wheeler might know? Really, Bel, such shabby behavior! And I suppose you haven't told him you're not a maid, either!"

"Nonsense," exclaimed, Isabel, lamely. "It's no matter what he believes. But maybe Corliss will go ahead and marry the colonel after all."

"You believe that?" Geoffrey looked at his sister with some contempt. He was learning that women saw what they wanted to see, he told himself. "Corliss won't marry him without spilling the whole scheme. She's more honest than we are, you know."

"Pooh!" said Isabel without conviction. "Corliss won't need to tell him, because she really is Corliss."

Geoffrey was still troubled. "No one will need to tell him," he said gloomily. "He knows."

"Knows that Corliss is Corliss? That's idiotic!"

"No it isn't! I wish you will listen to me, Isabel, when I'm talking instead of preening yourself in the mirror. Really, you don't know everything!"

Unconvinced, she said, with some scorn, "What is everything, then?"

"Everything is, that Colonel Renfrew was in the hall when that brother of Corliss's was shouting that she could go to the devil."

Isabel jumped from her chair. "He was in the foyer? Impossible! Where was Minch? He couldn't have let him in. He would have turned him away."

"No, he wouldn't. He was standing in the doorway, his big ears listening as hard as he could. I saw the colonel leaving the house. Just after Sir Ralph had shouted that she was none of his family!"

"All he meant was that he was disinheriting her!"

"Ah," said Geoffrey swiftly, "but it didn't sound like that, did it? Renfrew left as though he could not get away fast enough." Satisfied with Isabel's shocked reaction to his confidences, he added, "Who knows what he's thinking now?"

Isabel did not require time for reflection. It was as though she had known all along that that Grandmother's scheme required delicate walking on a frozen pond, above frigid depths that could swallow them all up. And now it had happened. They had made a mistake somewhere, and the ice had broken.

"The only way," she assured her brother, "to find out what he is thinking is to go and ask him."

"Go to his rooms?" Geoffrey was aghast. "Even an abigail can't do that!"

"I shall not go as an abigail. I have no doubt that what we have to say to him will go down much better if he knows we are his cousins."

"We! Bel, I absolutely forbid you to go see him!"

"Pooh! Geoffrey, go get out of that footman's livery, and I'll change. Don't you see? We've got to straighten it all out. For Corliss! She never wanted any part of this scheme. We owe her this, at least." She paused, reflecting. "Although I don't quite understand how it is that Grandmama chose a name out of a book, and it turned out to be Corliss's own. Ah well, Corliss told us downstairs just now that Meredith Havens was out of a book too."

"I wonder who she really is," said Geoffrey gloomily. "I misdoubt we've got to the bottom of it all even now."

"No matter. She ought to be Mrs. Renfrew, the way she looks at him. Go on, Geoffrey, move!"

She pushed him out the door, saying only, "There's no need for everyone to know what we're doing. Don't tell Grandmama."

With a rare flash of humor, Geoffrey said, "Don't worry, I'm not all that proud of this whole scheme!"

Isabel hurried to her small wardrobe, and after some thought decided upon a pomona green walking dress, with a poke bonnet lined with green silk to match. She looked at herself in the mirror, with admiring eyes. The hat made her look entirely grown-up, and she blessed her grandmother's mistake that had thought it suitable for Corliss. Even in Corliss's hand-me-down, so to speak, Isabel knew she looked stunning enough to astonish Captain Wheeler. She'd show him she was no parlor maid!

Half an hour later, strolling down the street toward Pulteney's, Isabel appeared to be precisely what she was—a young lady of good family taking a walk escorted by her brother. Totally unexceptionable, as she was required to tell Geoffrey more than once.

Her heart did not fail her until they arrived within sight of the hotel. It was a handsome building faced with square blocks of stone. A balcony over the main entrance overlooked the street. The fashionable establishment was of course an entirely respectable place to visit, but her apprehension was based on the recollection that Corliss's brother must surely be staying here, as well.

Upstairs, the colonel looked at the note that Isabel had sent up. "Charles! Pray read this and tell me what it means."

"An ill-writ note, you notice. Therefore, a young lady of education and breeding, with small grasp of literacy."

"Charles . . ."

"Miss Isabel Garnett? Who is she?"

"I cannot think. Lady Jarman's daughter is Mrs. Garnett, but there is no Miss Garnett—unless, Miss Hewett . . . ?"

Douglas had told his friend about the stir in Lady Jarman's salon. He had not liked to admit that he had been eavesdropping, even though unintentionally, but his mood when he returned to their rooms was evidence that something out of the ordinary had occurred. "Besides," Douglas told him, "we may wish not to intrude on the family until we have a better idea of the problem."

"Intrude?" said Charles, his eyebrows rising. "My only interest is that pert maid who beguiles me. Do I take it then that you are breaking off your pursuit of Miss Hewett? Whoever she may be! I had quite thought we would read an interesting announcement within the week!"

Slowly, Douglas shook his head. "Not breaking off, of course. She is—too important to me. But it is foolhardy to take cavalry across broken ground and jump hedges when you don't know what lies just beyond. But I don't know just how to find out what trouble she is in."

Now, Isabel's note in hand, Douglas's spirits rose. "I think, Charles, I should like it if you were to escort them up. Perhaps we have the answer to Corliss's troubles right in our hands."

When the door opened to admit Isabel and Geoffrey, Douglas was intrigued by the very odd expression on his friend's features. But that explanation must wait. Just now, he was forced to entertain some very odd notions himself.

"But—you are . . ." He glanced at the note which he still held. "Miss Isabel Garnett? But I recognize you, I think."

"I told you, Bel," began Geoffrey, in an agony of embarrassment.

"I can explain." Isabel was severely daunted, but the only way to accomplish what she had come for was to forge ahead. She lifted her chin and said, "Do you always keep your guests standing, Colonel Renfrew?"

Quickly, chairs were found, and they sat. Douglas kept his eyes fixed on the girl—surely he had seen her before? He noticed that Charles stared at her, too, with an unreadable, but unaccountably stern, expression.

The answer came to Douglas. "You're the parlor maid!"

"Yes, and that is what I—we—this is my brother Geoffrey, you know—came to tell you."

"Very well," said Douglas, beginning to think he might as well be entertained by this untoward visit, since he did not understand any of it. "You will tell me that you are a parlor maid. And I do recognize your footman. And then?"

"Well, first of all," said Isabel, encouraged by their reception—at least, they had been admitted to Colonel Renfrew's sitting-room. The rest, she thought erroneously, would be easier— "First of all, I should perhaps refer to you as Cousin Douglas."

"Should you indeed?"

"Yes, for my father was George Garnett, and that makes us cousins. And of course, you know about that infamous will, and that caused all the trouble. And Grandmama said the only way to get the money that should be ours after the odious Mr. Ackley was so rude was to . . ." Once started, Isabel found it difficult to stop. "And Corliss had to change her name although she was Corliss all the time and we didn't know it, and she didn't want to any of the time but Grandmama—"

Douglas interrupted ruthlessly. "The infamous will? And what has Mr. Ackley to do with anything? I do not understand. The only money I have inherited was entailed. I had no choice, you know."

"Not *that* money. The other money."

Douglas Renfrew had not dealt with subalterns for some years without gaining a bit of experience. "Best start," he said now, with a firmness that had its effect on both Isabel and Geoffrey, "at the beginning."

Under his skillful hand, the story emerged. Mrs. Garnett's fruitless visit to Douglas's agent Mr. Ackley was narrated, the unentailed legacy that would come to the Garnetts once Douglas was betrothed was explained, the whole foolish scheme of impersonation to lead him to a betrothal—

"And all Corliss—that is, Miss Hewett—had in mind was to accept my offer and then cry off?"

Charles looked up quickly, his attention caught by the pain in his friend's voice.

"Yes—that is, no—"

"Bel," interrupted Geoffrey, "you're making a mull of this. I knew you would."

He had not spoken so far, so the sound of his voice startled the others. Bel recovered enough to say, "Very well, then, you tell it."

"The thing is, sir, we talked about sending word to you to ask you to consider turning over the money that came from your grandmother, that is—"

"The unentailed part of the estate," prompted Douglas. "I did not know about this provision."

"But we did not know your direction. And Mr. Ackley insulted my mother, so you see of course we could not go back to him to inquire. Merry—that is, Corliss—did not want to do it. But Grandmama insisted. It takes a strong will to resist her, I can tell you. She told Corliss how much she owed to us—all nonsense, of course, all we did was to take her in when she hurt her ankle—and then I think she found out her brother had got married and she didn't know anything about it. At least, that's what she said today in the salon. You heard her, sir."

"Not the whole of it," Douglas told him. "So that was all she wanted—"

Isabel broke in. "Oh, no, sir. She's been most unhappy. She did like you, sir, I know for a fact. And she still does."

There was much to digest in the tales of these two children, and Douglas was not ready to pronounce judgment. Instead, he stalled for time.

"What do you think, Charles?"

"I think, Douglas, that these two infants—for surely Miss Garnett cannot be above fourteen—"

"I'm sixteen!"

"These two infants," he repeated, "have played at being servants for so long that, once given permission to talk, they spout enormous amounts of fustian!" So saying, Charles left them, shutting the door to an inner room with some force. Charles, thought Douglas, was excessively angry. But Douglas doubted that the infamous will and its consequences were the cause.

iii

After the young Garnetts had left, escorted by
their host to the lobby, Douglas went back to his
rooms upstairs. There were serious gaps in the
story he had just heard, which could be explained
by the probability that the family elders—Mrs.
Garnett and Lady Jarman—had been discreet in
their private discussions.

He did not for a moment doubt the truth of the
incidents they had told him, since much was explained thereby. But there were still some nagging
doubts—for instance, the position of Sir Ralph
Hewett, Corliss's brother, in the scheme. He seemed
to be only a marplot. However, Douglas had heard
him say, "You're none of my family!"

Did he mean that literally? Or was he disinheriting her, as Isabel believed? Apparently there was
little love lost between the Hewetts, since Sir Ralph
had not even told his sister that he was marrying.

There were other questions in Douglas's mind.
One he could try to have answered immediately.
He crossed to knock on Charles's door.

"They've gone, Charles. Come on out and ad-
vise me."

In a moment the door opened and Charles
emerged. His ordinarily pleasant face was set in
dour lines, and his eyes were miserable. His first
words were, "That damned minx!" and his second
were, "What am I going to do, Douglas? She's a
school miss, of apparently impeccable breeding!"

Instead of receiving advice from his friend, Douglas found that he himself was called on to play the role of comforter.

"Don't tell me you are serious about the young lady!" said Douglas, in an attempt to lighten his mood. "You're only after little serving maids, you told me!"

"Shut up!" said Charles savagely, and in a moment his mood altered, and he said, "The girl is sixteen, Douglas. Give her a year at home, and another year in London, and then—in two years, Douglas!—I may be able to offer to her. If no one else strikes her fancy in the interval. I know I'm years older than she is, and—as long as I thought she was a parlor maid—"

"Don't tell me you are disappointed to find out she is not, for I won't believe you. You could not be hit so hard if she were only a whim of the moment."

Charles had never looked less like a military man. He leaned forward in his chair, his hands clasped between his knees and his head down, apparently studying the design of the carpet. Rose-petal skin, golden curls, blue eyes—Isabel possessed everything he had dreamed of under the hot Spanish skies, as well as a bright intelligence, and now he could not have her for two years, if then.

"Very well, Douglas," he said at last, feeling his friend's silence weighing on him. "What's all this about a will, and Ackley? You were not pleased with him, I think you said? Is the girl telling the truth?"

"I think she must be," said Douglas slowly, "for no one in her right mind could make up such a taradiddle. If she is right, and there is such a legacy, one I can dispose of, I shall of course do it. I received word only that the old man had died and I had got the lot. Ackley did not tell me that there was unentailed capital, or in fact any details at all." He thought a moment. "He will, of course, be required to account for his abominable treatment of Mrs. Garnett."

"He won't give you the truth."

"He must inform me about my inheritance, and show me my ancestor's will. That, at least, cannot be distorted. It seems my grandmother's dowry was not part of the entail, although he controlled the disposition of it. I have been too preoccupied with—with other matters—to deal with business." Douglas rose. "I think I shall call on Mr. Ackley at once. If he is engaged, he will simply have to interrupt his interview to deal with me."

"Shall I go with you?"

"No, I thank you." He surveyed his friend carefully. "If I may suggest something, Charles? Could you call on Lady Jarman and tell her your wishes about young Miss Garnett? I admit I am wondering whether a London Season will appeal to that young lady. She may be sixteen as she says, but she is as forthright as any dowager!"

The sudden light in Charles's eyes reassured Douglas, and he left to visit his agent, determined to find out the truth of the notorious will, and to have the pleasure of dismissing the man who had insulted Mrs. Garnett.

Later, as he rose to leave the scruffy office of the man his grandfather had entrusted with his affairs, Douglas said, "I wish the initial payment of the interest on the sums we spoke of to be forwarded at once to Mrs. Garnett. You may wait upon her tomorrow at Lady Jarman's in Hanover Square."

"But, she will have to sign papers, there are formalities—"

"I trust you will find ways to expedite this transfer. As, of course, you will prepare your books and statements ready to turn over to my new agent."

Mr. Ackley, unused to such treatment as he had just now suffered, being more adapted to dealing with petitioning ladies of little financial education, faltered, "New agent. Of course, sir. Excellent." When he later realized that he had lost a remunerative account, he could not believe his own folly.

"I am on my way now," added Douglas, "to Hanover Square myself to inform my cousin of my actions. I shall tell her she will hear from you tomorrow."

Convinced now of the major truths contained in Isabel's explanation, Douglas Renfrew proceeded to Lady Jarman's to impart the news of his dispositions to Mrs. Garnett. He was walking much better now, he realized, having given no thought to his supporting cane for several weeks. The fever would from time to time come back, he was sure, that being its nature, but at least he could believe he would become his old self again, and might even learn to enjoy his removal to the ancestral home, after the tumultuous years at war.

But could he enjoy anything if Corliss were not with him? He had recognized that he was greatly attracted to her, indeed intended to offer for her in due time. Now, knowing that she was in trouble, of whatever kind, his attraction turned into a full-fledged and insistent need. Whatever Corliss had done, even in agreeing to entrap him and then, so Isabel said, cry off, now made no difference to him.

Although he was aware of feeling a deep hurt that she had not confided in him, he was also conscious that there was no way she could have done so without betraying the Garnetts. But whatever she had done, she must have had good reason for it. A factor in his arrival at this conclusion was the recollection of that loud, overbearing voice that had shouted within Lady Jarman's salon—shouted at Corliss? Whatever means she needed to take to remove herself from that awful man were justified indeed.

At Lady Jarman's he asked not for Corliss—to Minch's surprise—but for Mrs. Garnett. In a short time, she joined him in the salon, and crossed the room, holding out her hand to him.

"How nice of you to call, Douglas! Perhaps Minch was mistaken, and you asked for dear Corliss? Nonetheless, I am delighted to see you! Shall we sit over here?"

Following her to the designated chairs, he realized that she had no idea of Isabel's and Geoffrey's visit to him. He should have recognized the likelihood that the precious pair were acting on their own. No one responsible could have countenanced such a visit. But now, it came to him, he could not betray them. He had a need to improvise, and that quickly.

"I asked particularly for you. I have finally found time to take care of some business that I should have dealt with before this. I collect that you have been informed about my great-grandfather's will—your late husband's ancestor too, of course?"

"Yes," she replied, slightly distressed. "I cannot think why he could have cut out my husband so cruelly."

"I don't think," said Douglas, newly informed of all the circumstances, "it was a case of cutting George out. After all, he had already married, and very happily too, I am sure. I was the only brand left to be snatched from the burning. My regret is that I was in Spain when he died, and thus I did not know about that part of the will until today."

That at least was true. Isabel had opened his eyes only hours earlier.

Feeling that brevity and swiftness were the most humane ways of dealing with his news for her, he told her in only a few words. She was, as he had expected, stunned. Fortunately, she did not think to inquire as to the source of his information about Mr. Ackley's insults, letting her think, if she would, that the man himself had boasted of them.

"And," he finished, letting her have time to recover from the news that she would have the entire capital of the bequest and not simply the interest, and that she would have no money worries from this point on, "I suggest that you do not use Mr. Ackley as your agent."

She roused from her trance enough to say, "Certainly not! I cannot abide the man!"

"I have myself determined that I have no more use for him, and I have told him so. But there are certain formalities that must be gotten through, so he will wait upon you tomorrow. With, I may say, the first payment of interest due you. Of course, the transfer of the capital will follow. I could not date the transfer back to the date of the old man's demise. I'm sorry."

Gently, he sent her out of the room, still dazed with happiness and much relief, and asked her to tell Corliss he wished to see her.

Damn the man Ackley! he thought as he waited for Corliss. All the trouble the man had caused in his negligence and self-centered arrogance. He could have written to me, thought Douglas, told me about that foolish will drawn up to strike back at the woman who had married him and, no doubt for excellent reasons, left him. Instead, the victims were Margaret Garnett, a pleasant and sweet-natured woman, and those children.

He had never thought to ask about any younger children. There must be some, however, perhaps left in the country. Judging from the way that family conducted its affairs, he would not be too surprised to learn that they were all acting as kitchen maids or stable boys. Isabel had dropped a remark about—not just for Geoffrey and me, but for the others!

Finally, it came to him that he had been waiting an inordinately long time for Corliss. Surely she would not have to spend hours getting dressed to see him. His visit was not a formal one, and she did not usually make him wait.

But when Minch entered the room, Douglas could see by the expression on his face that he was the bearer of bad news.

"Miss Hewett is not receiving today, sir."

Douglas was deeply disappointed. "Perhaps to-morrow, then. Pray inform her that I shall call in the afternoon with the hope of seeing her then."

Minch's solemn expression grew more grave. "I have been asked to say, sir," he informed Douglas, with an air of disassociating himself from the information, "that Miss Hewett does not wish to receive you at any time."

Stunned to the anguished core, Douglas said an automatic thank-you and moved swiftly through the hall and out the front door.

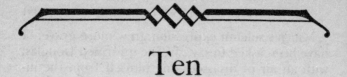

Ten

i

Try as she might, Lady Dacre could not erase from her mind the features of the girl who called herself Corliss Hewett. There was something familiar, almost haunting about the young lady. Elizabeth Dacre could not quite put her finger on the element that disturbed her.

She went over in her thoughts the entire episode in Hanover Square, from the moment the butler had admitted her. She knew Lady Jarman by reputation, and there was not the slightest smell of scandal about the woman. Lady Dacre had not been made privy to the underlying motive for the scheme, of course. All she knew was that a young lady was at this moment masquerading under the name of Lady Dacre's own cousin. And if this girl were not Corliss, then where was Corliss?

Elizabeth Dacre did not know where to start to trace Corliss on her journey. She could not understand the loss of a young lady, her abigail, her attendants, her brother's coach, and a pair of horses, possibly four. Perhaps Ralph would have an answer.

But in the meantime, she was reluctant to leave Portland Place until she was more settled in her mind. There was something about the girl, whom she had seen for just those few moments in the foyer, that seemed to be telling her something she ought to know.

First, the girl had looked to be unutterably happy. The light in the dark blue eyes had been prompted, doubtless, by the company of the gentleman who followed her into the entrance hall. But radiant as she appeared, Lady Dacre thought she detected a hint of unhappiness, a kind of haunting sadness in those eyes.

Lady Dacre searched her memory for a feature, even one feature, that reminded her of Fanny. There was nothing, not even those dark blue eyes, for Fanny's had been hazel. But in one or two Monteiths every generation had appeared eyes of that hue, as witness her own eyes—the Monteith blue! Could it be a coincidence? Too many coincidences here, she thought.

Elizabeth Dacre closed her own eyes to bring up from her recollection every detail of that meeting. The fashionable bonnet, the blue walking dress, the—the *brooch!* It was Fanny's brooch, belonging to her grandmother, Elizabeth's own aunt. An old-fashioned piece of jewelry, consisting of a large opal set round with garnets.

The girl was Corliss indeed! The brooch proved it. But why would Lady Jarman lie? There must be more than met the eye, and she was determined to get to the bottom of it.

She must see the girl again, and alone this time. She was obviously not a prisoner, or if she were, incarceration did not weigh heavily on her. Lady Jarman could not refuse to let Corliss visit Lady Dacre. Elizabeth would write a note and invite the girl to Portland Place.

Having done so, she gave the missive to Towne to deliver. "Hanover Square, Towne, the house at the center of the west side. You do not need to wait for an answer."

"Very well, my lady." Towne studied the super-scription, her expression altering as though she had drunk a dose of vinegar. "But if this young miss is not your cousin, my lady, then who is she? Are we to take strangers into our house, foreign-ers that like as not will murder us in our beds?"

"Foreigners, Towne? How ridiculous! That fam-ily is as English as we are."

"They're from London, not Yorkshire, ma'am." She caught her mistress's eye, and was warned. "Very well, ma'am," she repeated, and left the room.

She had almost gone too far with Lady Dacre, she realized, and vowed to watch her step for a while. There was more than one way to deal with this upstart, who wasn't even a real cousin. She would have been alarmed had she seen the specu-lation in Lady Dacre's eyes after she was left alone.

Towne left Portland Place and emerged on New Cavendish Street. She stumped along in her heavy boots in a countrywoman's stride. These walks were not made for honest folk, she decided, and the sooner they were all back at Dacre Hall the better they would all be. And without this Miss Corliss, or whoever she was. Lady Dacre had confided the details of her visit to Lady Jarman to her maid, and Towne had secretly rejoiced at her mistress's disappointment. Now it seemed, thought Towne, the whole thing was not yet finished. Her mood grew darker.

By the time Towne reached the round park in the center of Cavendish Square, she was trembling with anger, with jealousy, with the helpless fear of a woman whose future was suddenly threatened. Emerging from the square, instead of going directly on her way to Hanover Square, she veered onto Oxford Street and turned right.

How much better would it be if they had never heard of Corliss Hewett! Towne looked down at the letter she held in her hand. Temptation prodded her. She had never yet disobeyed a direct order of Lady Dacre's, but now her whole future was in the balance, she thought. A new cousin, genuine or not, who captured Lady Dacre's affection might well expect to inherit substantially. And Towne's own legacy would, through no fault of her own, be reduced by that same amount.

Towne was an uneducated woman of narrow intelligence. She knew her sums, she told herself, and what would go to Miss Corliss could not go to Towne. She did not know how long she walked, but by the time she reached Orchard Street, she turned right again to return to Portland Place. The streets, except at the crossings where they were swept, were full of debris. She stood for a long moment, considering tearing up the letter into small pieces and dropping the fragments into the teeming litter in the street. But suppose someone saw her? She could not take the chance. Much better to hide the telltale document somewhere in her room—under her thin mattress perhaps—until she found an unattended blaze in a fireplace, later in the season.

She thrust the letter into a pocket and hurried back to Portland Place, in a much better mood than when she had started on her errand.

ii

"Women! I will never understand women!"

Sir Ralph Hewett paced the floor of the sitting room he had hired in Pulteney's Hotel.

"That is true," said Lady Hewett, "as long as you roar like a lion and never listen to them."

He stopped short. "Listen?" he demanded. "Listen to what? To her telling me to go to the devil? My own sister? Well, what do you say to that?"

"I suspect you suggested it first, Ralph. But when you are ready to sit down and talk, I have something to say."

Like a sail spilling its wind, Ralph felt deflated. There was nothing his common-born wife could tell him, he thought. But in the few weeks since his marriage, he had been surprised on more than one occasion by her shrewd observations. If he had not given her credit, at least he had seen their value, and quietly instituted her suggestions as though they were his own.

Hearing his own bluster subsiding, he stood, back to the window, feet planted far apart, and said, "I suppose you know just what will bring Corliss to her senses? You don't even know the girl."

Theresa, recognizing Ralph's words for the futile thrusts they were, said, "You're going about this the wrong way. You said she was distressed not to know about our marriage? Then, she will not listen to anything you have to say. Your only hope is to enlist Lady Dacre's assistance. She can reach the girl. I should imagine your sister will not receive you again at Lady Jarman's."

At least I wouldn't, thought Theresa Hewett. She was beginning to believe that the title she had longed for was exacting an excessively high price. If it weren't for the advantages she expected to accrue to Phyllida, she would chuck the lot and go home to Birmingham.

Her suggestions made good sense, Ralph thought. Besides, it was Lady Dacre's fault too, for not writing to him when Corliss did not arrive.

He said as much to Lady Dacre in her salon, not much later. Adjured by his hostess to sit down and stop pacing like a lion in the Tower, he was perched on the edge of a chair, leaning forward to look accusingly into her face.

Lady Hewett sat carefully on a chair a little removed, and looked around her. If Ralph had paid little heed to the elegance of this house, she was far more observant, and even a bit envious. No matter how she redid the ancestral manor of the Hewetts, regardless of how much money she poured into the project, she would not have a touch adequate to produce a room of quiet elegance and harmony such as this one.

Perhaps Corliss might be induced to assist?

Theresa realized the trend of her thoughts. She blamed Corliss much less for leaving her home—

and Ralph—than she had before. She had not yet
met Ralph's half-sister, but she was willing to like
her at once.

When she came back to the present, she saw
that Ralph was still setting forth his position.

"You know, of course, that it is Corliss over in
that house? I've seen her. We've had this entire
trip to London and all the upset, and for what? If
you had let me know that Corliss had not arrived,
I could have made inquiries of the stagecoach
company, and I would have found her, no doubt
of that!"

Color drained from Lady Dacre's face. "Stagecoach? I must believe you misspoke, Sir Ralph. On
my part, I have wondered why you did not realize
that something was amiss when your own carriage
and servants returned without dear Corliss."

"My carriage? I couldn't spare it, for I went to
Bath for my wedding."

"Then—forgive me if I seem to insist, but I do
not trust my understanding of this affair. You did
not send Corliss on the public stage, Sir Ralph, you
could not!" The expression on his face answered
her doubts. "You did! No wonder Corliss— But I
suppose her abigail—" She eyed him with clear
disgust. "Of course, no abigail. No wonder the
child did not write you. She must have felt entirely abandoned by everyone she knew. Sir Ralph,
all I can say is—" She drew herself up to a formidable posture and allowed the contempt she felt
for him to be evident. "I did my best to keep dear
Fanny from marrying your father. Now I see I
did not nearly enough, for you are as like him
as two peas."

She glanced at Theresa. "My condolences on

your marriage, my dear." She raised her voice slightly. "Flint!"

The butler was in the room at once. "Pray show Sir Ralph and Lady Hewett out."

No wonder, thought Lady Dacre when she was alone again, Corliss had fallen into uncomfortable circumstances. No abigail, riding a public stage— Lady Dacre shuddered at the thought—and doubtless with as little money as amounted to none.

And while she wished to hear precisely how Corliss had arrived in Lady Jarman's hands, having started out in a stagecoach, she could begin to be grateful to that lady for coming to Corliss's rescue. At least she was regarded as a young lady of quality, and not a kitchen maid!

But why had Corliss given a false name at the start? And why had Lady Jarman brought her to London? There was a taradiddle about arranging a good match for her . . .

Well, by now Towne should have delivered the letter to Corliss, and she could expect to hear soon from the girl's own lips exactly what had happened to her.

iii

Sir Ralph was not the only gentleman in London to give vent to his feelings by pacing the floor. Colonel Renfrew also strode back and forth in his parlor, pausing to look from the window into the street from time to time.

"Good God, Douglas!" exclaimed Charles, fi-

nally reaching the limit of his tolerance. "You'll
have the carpet in shreds!"

Charles was in the sulks himself, Douglas knew.
He refrained from remarking on his friend's blue-
deviled mood, because he knew full well the cause,
and only time could ease his burden. Two years'
time before Miss Garnett would be eligible to receive Charles's advances, and as any soldier from
the Peninsula could tell you, there was no guaran-
tee of tomorrow, to say nothing of twenty-four
months.

Charles forced himself to consider his friend.
"She won't see you? Give her time. She'll come
around. I wager in two days you may well find her
delighted to receive you. Be sure to send me a
card to your wedding!"

"You idiot!" said Douglas without rancor.

"You don't think you'll win her? I tell you—"

"Only one thing I want you to tell me, Charles,"
said the colonel, a light of sudden determination
in his gray eyes. "I've got to talk to her, in private.
I must get her away from the family that I fear
has gulled her into the scheme of bringing me up
to the mark. I can't believe she is anything but a
tool in the hands of Lady Jarman."

"You're speaking of your own cousins, Douglas?
Although I should imagine that most families have
some members about whom they have reservations."

"Lady Jarman is no kin of mine. Her daughter
married my cousin George, that is the only connection. I want your opinion, Charles. What do
you think of this? I'll hire a carriage, and wait
until she leaves the house—"

Charles gaped. "You're speaking about an ab-
duction? I think you're on the right track. How-

ever, I suggest that we go about this in a methodical fashion. Planning makes all the difference to success, you know."

"You're looking at me very oddly, Charles. You have a plan?"

Charles, noting the feverish shine in the familiar gray eyes, was uneasy. He suspected that the illness that had brought them both back to England—with such unhappy results!—might well have Douglas in its grip again.

"Well? I believe I must take strong measures. If she sees me and tells me herself she wishes no more of me, I must accept her decision. What do you suggest?"

Charles, with an air of great resolution, said, "First I think we must raid Manton's, perhaps tonight."

"Manton's? The gunsmith?"

"Think, Douglas. You have a carriage into which you force the lady you love, regardless of her wishes. You carry her off, and Lady Jarman will send the Bow Street runners after you, and you can imagine what the duke will say? An officer of his headquarters staff, standing trial at the Old Bailey for heinous crimes? Of course, we will need armament from Manton's. That cane of yours won't deal with more than one of the runners."

"I thought you were serious!"

"I was never more serious in my life. A carriage into which you may entice the lady—but then what? Suppose she screams, as she might well do. Douglas, you've had your regiment too long. England lives by different rules, you know. The only hope is to wait for her to change her mind."

"I cannot. I feel that time is the enemy. She is in trouble of some kind."

"That foolish scheme that Miss Garnett told us of? Isn't that trouble enough?"

"No, I cannot agree. She was in some kind of trouble before, or she would never have become a party to Lady Jarman's plot."

"A plot that was unnecessary all the time."

"Ackley did me a mischief on that score. But you are wrong, Charles, she will not reconsider. She returned my note unopened. The butler said she did not want to see me again, ever. But if she needs help, then I must be at hand."

"But suppose," said Charles, with an air of shrewdness, "that her background is such as to make her ineligible to marry you?"

"I will marry her anyway," said Douglas simply. "If she will have me."

He got to his feet, and went to the window to look down into the street.

"What do you expect to see? Miss Hewett?"

Douglas considered that question did not deserve an answer, so he gave none. But he resumed his pacing back and forth, lost in unproductive reflections.

"Go out, Douglas. Walk on the pavement. Walk to the Tower. Walk to Canterbury, for all I care. But have some pity on my poor head, which is beginning to ache from all this violence in the very air."

It was a good idea, thought Douglas. He knew he would suffer another sleepless night if he did not dispel his excessive nervous energy. Grabbing his hat and stick, he went downstairs into the lobby. There was a gentleman of ordinary appearance but testy mood just outside the manager's office. A well-dressed, frowning lady stood beside him, as he consulted with the manager.

"You're sure you have no message for me," the gentleman was demanding, as though his next step would be to invade the manager's premise and rummage for himself.

Douglas paused. Surely he had heard that voice before? Was it not the same voice that had streamed loudly from Lady Jarman's salon? It was, and this must be the same person who had claimed that Corliss was no relation of his. Douglas liked him no better now that he had seen him than he had before.

"Quite sure, Sir Ralph."

As soon as Ralph moved away, Douglas spoke to the manager quietly. "Is that Sir Ralph Hewett?"

The manager's nod confirmed Douglas in his surmise. He watched Sir Ralph and his lady, talking to each other, stroll toward the stairs. He did not try to listen, of course, which was as well since only a word or two were audible to him.

This was no place for a confrontation. If it turned out that Corliss could be induced to marry him, and that Sir Ralph was indeed the head of her family, then there would be no choice but to seek the man's permission to marry his sister. The colonel's features set in harsh lines as he strode through the lobby and onto the walk. The man would give his permission, or Douglas would—

He recognized the uncivilized direction his wild fancies took, and knew that Charles had the right of it. He had never felt so primitive, even in the

face of the life-or-death, blood-boiling advance
against French cavalry.

By the time he had walked as far as Brook
Street, where he had a notion of diverting his
thoughts with the latest journals in his club library, he found he was thinking the oddest thing.
Lady Dacre consumed his thoughts. Not the lady
herself, of course, for he did not know her at all.
But her name had wheeled into his consciousness
like a comet whirling across the sky.

Lady Dacre! Who could she be?

Once inside the club, he hesitated. He was un-
sure of the importance of that name to him, or
why it would have come to him. He had not even
picked up a journal, so the name could not have
been something he had seen in the news.

Then, as he was about to give it up, he remembered. Sir Ralph and Lady Hewett, walking across
the lobby in the hotel— She had said in an acri-
monious tone,"It's not Lady Dacre's fault . . ." *Fault?*
there must have been more— At last, he had it.
". . . that Corliss disappeared." That was it!

He paused only long enough to make inquiries
in his club, and then set out to call on Lady Dacre.

The civil thing would be to write her a note,
begging an interview, and then wait in patience
for her reply.

The polite way was not the way of Colonel
Renfrew.

At Portland Place, he said to the butler, "Lady
Dacre does not know me, but I would be most
grateful if she could see me for a few moments."

To his enormous surprise, before the butler
could even beckon a footman to take his hat and
stick, a small, comfortably padded woman sailed

into the hall from an open door on the right. Not a young woman, for her hair was streaked with gray, but her eyes were youthful, he saw. And they were of the same dark blue color as his dear Corliss's eyes!

He knew then that he had seen her before, when he brought Corliss home—this was the lady who had been passing through the hall when Corliss had fainted! And not from the sun, as he had supposed, but from something connected with this lady. I am moving a step closer to the solution of this mystery, he thought with relief.

Lady Dacre offered her hand, and he bent over it. "I must say that it is so fortunate that you came to call on me. I have wanted to speak to you, but I had not your direction, and I did not wish to ask anyone."

Mystified, Douglas followed her into the salon, a light room of mostly soft greens and golds.

"I do not understand," he said when they were both seated. "We have not met, it is true, but I know now where I have seen you. I think we have a mutual acquaintance in Lady Jarman?"

"Oh, yes, of course. And you are the mysterious colonel that Philomena told me about when she wrote about dear Corliss. The letter, you know, that brought me to London to find out what had happened to the girl."

"I have heard some of the story," he said earnestly, "but I would be in your debt if you were to tell me the whole of it."

"First let me ask you, have you met that dreadful half-brother of hers? Sir Ralph Hewett?"

"Not to say met," said Douglas. "But I have seen him. And heard him."

"Believe me, my dear colonel, further acquaintance does not improve him. Well, you see, Corliss's mother and I quarreled some years ago. Ralph's father, Sir Gervase, was just such another as Ralph, and I begged Fanny not to marry him."

She was well-launched on her narrative. Douglas interrupted her only once, to ask, "You are her guardian, perhaps?"

"No. But in six months she will be of age, or is it next year? Soon anyway."

"It is of no use asking your permission to marry Corliss, then?"

"Before you have heard her story?"

He quite liked this old lady, and that same sweet smile that turned Corliss's heart over had much the same effect on her cousin Elizabeth. "Before, or after, I shall marry her in the end."

"Then," said Lady Dacre, leaning forward and touching his knee lightly with her fingers, "then between us we can manage Ralph."

Her narrative, shorn of her comments and diversionary remarks, was short. He found himself not appalled, for Corliss had merely taken the best way out of a dilemma not of her own making, and showed remarkably good sense in so doing, but conscious of a rising fury that could most easily be eased by the simple throttling of his girl's insufferable brother.

Lady Dacre was still speaking. "I have recently sent an invitation to Corliss to come to tea this afternoon. I expect her momentarily, even though she did not write an answer."

The recollection of that other occasion when Corliss had not written brought a frown to her forehead. "Perhaps, colonel, you will wait a moment while I inquire."

Flint, summoned, was of no help. "No, my lady, no message has come of which I am aware." His expression indicated that any message daring to enter the house unbeknownst to him would have short shrift. Then a thought occurred to him. Always suspicious of his lady's maid, and fully reciprocating Towne's dislike of him, he recalled that she had been strangely quiet the last couple of days.

"Perhaps Towne could inform you, my lady?"

"Oh, no," said Lady Dacre. "She would have told me." But she too remembered Towne's odd manner. "Perhaps you would ask her to come."

Towne had spent a wretched two days since she had returned home, her mission unfulfilled. She had put the telltale letter under her mattress. Believing she could see a slight elevation above the letter, she had moved it to the back of a drawer, and then, dissatisfied, to a pocket of a cloak she seldom wore.

Flint, scenting excitement of a kind, sedately climbed the stairs to the top floor, rather than sending a maid. As he stopped in the open door, he saw Towne standing in the center of the small room, an envelope in her hand, and an unmistakable look of guilt on her face.

Towne had read her fate in the glint of triumph in the butler's eyes. Fortunately she had put a little by, in her years of well paid service, and her sister in Scarborough would be glad to take her in, if not for her person then for her expected contributions to the household.

"You'll be out of the house by tomorrow," gloated Flint, "and no use to go running to Lady Dacre. I wonder you'd have nerve enough to face her!"

Towne didn't. She looked down the long years ahead, and knew what it was to feel regret.

iv

Corliss, immured in her wretchedness as in a prison, was not aware of other events taking place around her. She had refused to see Colonel Renfrew, suspecting that the mere sight of him would undo all her resolutions.

Lady Dacre had denied her, there in the hall. "Poor child," she had said with great pity, but no recognition. She was sure that Cousin Elizabeth had dropped her from her thoughts, believing her to be an imposter.

Corliss did not know, either, that Douglas had overheard the argument in the salon with Ralph. But she knew that Ralph had denied her then, disowned her in front of the entire Garnett family and the butler Minch. "You are none of *my* family!" he had shouted, a remark that was susceptible of more than one interpretation.

Corliss, uncharacteristically filled with gloom, believed she had been disowned, so to speak, irrevocably. She would not, could not go to Douglas under such a cloud.

The third day, she left her room and sought the company of the Garnetts. She still kept her affection for Mrs. Garnett and Isabel, and the other children. Lady Jarman, however, would have been well advised not to presume on Corliss's supposed liking of her.

Corliss started down the stairs, thinking idly how odd everything looked, even though nothing had been changed in three days. Nothing but Corliss herself, she thought sadly. I will never be the same.

When she reached the main hall, she stopped to listen. There were no servants in the hall, since it was quite early in the day and no callers might be expected. Voices came from the breakfast room, through the door at the back of the hall, and she started in that direction. When she heard her own name pronounced—her real name—she stopped short.

Lady Jarman's voice came clearly, obviously answering a previous speaker. "We have what we came to London for, and I confess it is most generous of dear Douglas to turn the entire estate in question over to you. I cannot think how he came to do it, for it surely could not be the doing of that odious man Ackley. Did he explain to you, Margaret?"

"No, Mama. He said only that he had just learned of the provisions of the will, and that was all."

"Well," said Lady Jarman with a sigh, "that was enough. There's nothing to keep us here in London any longer. I am sure you will wish to return home, Margaret, and I am anxious to close this house."

"But the Little Season?" It was Isabel's voice.

Corliss added eavesdropping to her other recently acquired faults, and did not move.

"You are too young," said Lady Jarman in a tone that admitted of no appeal.

"Besides," said Geoffrey, "you've said often enough that you don't want a Season."

"I don't," said Isabel. "But as long as we are here—"

"But we are not here for long. In a sennight, this house will be empty again."

Then came Isabel's voice again. "But where will Corliss go?"

There was a measurable silence. In the hall, Corliss held her breath. The answer was of some moment to her.

"Good God," said Lady Jarman in a chastened voice, "I forgot entirely about her."

"Grandmama, how could you—!"

Forgot? Lady Jarman *forgot* her?

Corliss had come to the end of it all—her constant whipping herself up to do the right thing for the Garnetts, her intense love for Douglas and the conviction he would turn away in disgust when he found out she had lied, and lied. But the worst of it was that she was aware of a deep chasm in her own thoughts—an abyss that she had not dared to think about until now. She did not know what would become of her if Douglas failed her ... and the Garnetts took up their own impecunious life again ... and, oh, what would become of her in the end?

She had believed that Lady Jarman thought kindly of her, and that Margaret had a strong affection for her—but now—

I forgot her—the abyss was a mere footstep away.

Corliss did not wait to hear more. Picking up her skirts, she ran upstairs, observed only by Minch through the baize door leading to the kitchens, and closed her door behind her. Her first reaction was to pick up a pillow from the nearest chair and throw it vigorously against the wall. The next pillow she hurled across the room onto the bed. When she picked up the next object, and felt the smooth porcelain of the lamp beneath her fingertips, she paused, and set it back on the table.

I haven't thrown anything since I was in my nursery, she recalled ruefully. But it is really too much! I thought that even if my family, who I suppose owes me little, deserted me, I would still have the good will and affection of these people who have become my second family!

I even introduced them to Ralph as "my new family"!

How could I have been so blind? I was a tool to them, no more. I was a means to an end—an idiot girl believing she could carry out a stratagem for her friends, her "new family," without suffering any hurt herself. Even, she thought, I must have expected some gratitude.

Now Lady Jarman, whose persuasive talents had overridden Corliss's objections, had entirely forgotten her. She had thought that perhaps the Garnetts would take her in, now that they were in funds, but that hope must be dashed, for Isabel had clearly expected her grandmother to provide for Corliss.

Well! thought Corliss, finally. No one is going to have to provide for Corliss Hewett! She did not know how she would go on, but she would think of something—she must!

But not in this house. She could not breathe in this musty room, now a stranger's room to her. She picked up a thin shawl, crammed a bonnet on her head with little heed, and slipped unseen out of the house.

She was not missed for an hour.

Not until Isabel carried breakfast upstairs to Corliss was it learned that she was not in her room. In moments, after Isabel made inquiries in the kitchen, it was found that she was no longer in the house—anywhere.

"Mama! Grandmama!" Isabel flew downstairs to spread the news.

"Too young for a Season, that's certain, Isabel, if you cannot control yourself better than that," reproved Lady Jarman.

"You don't understand," cried Isabel. "Corliss is gone!"

"Nonsense," said Lady Jarman. "She cannot be gone."

"She is, Grandmama. I asked in the kitchen, and they haven't seen her. I looked in all the bedrooms—"

"But you must not have looked carefully. Come, Margaret, you and I will find her. I had not expected her to cause us trouble in this way. She is in the house, somewhere."

I don't think so, thought Isabel. She had a real affection for Corliss, and was much concerned over Corliss's obvious misery. She must love Colonel Renfrew—Cousin Douglas, that is—very much, and although Isabel could not see a reason for her refusing even to see him, to say nothing of marrying him, no doubt her friend had her reasons.

As for Isabel, she would marry Captain Wheeler in a moment—if, of course, he ever asked her. She had seen him, that same day that she and Geoffrey had confessed everything to Douglas, standing across the square looking at the house. She had expected him to come to call, either on Mrs. Garnett or Lady Jarman, and she had carefully placed herself near the back of the entrance hall so he would be sure to see her when he entered the house. But after a while, when he did not come, she had looked across the square, and he was gone.

How she wished he were here right now! He would know what to do in this emergency. Isabel had no illusions as to the gravity of the situation. She had seen Corliss sit apathetically, face drawn, looking into space, these last days.

Her mother and grandmother returned to the hall. "She's not in the house at all," said Lady Jarman, as though announcing a discovery.

I told you that, thought Isabel mutinously.

Mrs. Garnett said thoughtfully, "You don't think she could have heard us talking about going home, do you? She could not have heard us from upstairs."

Minch cleared his throat. "If I may, my lady? Miss Hewett indeed overheard the conversation from the breakfast room. I observed her in the hall at that time."

"Good God!" cried Isabel, ignoring her mother's frown at her impulsive language. "She may have thrown herself in the river."

"Don't be absurd, Isabel!" scolded her grandmother. But an uneasy expression moved across her face, and she said, "We must find her at once. Geoffrey, you go in the direction of the river. The rest of you . . ."

As Geoffrey started out of the front door, Isabel grabbed his sleeve and followed him outside. "Geoffrey, I want you to do me a favor."

"I've got to go, Isabel. I can't stop."

"This will do more good than running after Corliss. Besides, I'll go to the river myself. You go to Pulteney's and tell—"

"No good telling Cousin Douglas. She'll run from him, most likely."

"I mean Captain Wheeler. He's the one we need. He'll know what to do."

She did not wait for his agreement, but flew out of the square in the direction of Westminster Bridge.

v

Geoffrey's news, imparted to the gentlemen in Pulteney's Hotel, startled them in diverse ways. As Geoffrey expected, Cousin Douglas sprang to his feet in surprise, but in moments his expression turned thoughtful. Geoffrey was oddly reminded of a coiled spring.

"Gone? But where did she go?"

"She didn't leave a note. Bel thought she might be going to the river. She's gone to look for her."

Charles Wheeler questioned Geoffrey closely. "You say she went toward the river? Was she alone?"

"I told you, sir, we do not know where she went. Nor when," he added for good measure.

"She should not be alone in those streets," fretted Charles.

"It's high noon, Charles, in the middle of a civilized city," said Douglas.

"I'll get a hackney, Douglas. You may go with me if you hurry, for I will not wait. Even now she could be in the clutches of some villain! You, Geoffrey, come with me!"

"No, Geoffrey," said Douglas in a tone of quiet command. "I need you."

Charles, not waiting to discuss the matter, vanished into the hall, and they could hear his swiftly descending footsteps.

"He's daft," muttered Geoffrey. "I told him we didn't know where Corliss went. How did he expect someone to go with her?"

Douglas was writing a note at the small desk. He looked up. "Oh, he didn't mean Corliss. Did you not know? He is worried about your sister."

"Bel?" cried Geoffrey skeptically.

In a moment Douglas had finished his note and, sealing it, gave it to Geoffrey. "Pray take this to Lady Dacre in Portland Place," he said. "When we find Corliss, she will not wish to go back to your house."

"I suppose not," said Geoffrey grudgingly. "But I thought she liked us."

"Quite likely she does." Douglas took the time to soothe his young cousin. "But something must have happened to make her leave the house, without a note, and without your sister."

"They said something at breakfast," confessed Geoffrey, "about going home. And Bel asked what Corliss was going to do, and nobody knew, and Corliss—at least Minch said so—overheard. She wouldn't eavesdrop!"

"An accident, doubtless. Nonetheless, we must find her."

"You think something could happen to her? Like Captain Wheeler thinks could happen to Bel?"

Douglas said, "We must find her before that occurs."

"Where will you be, sir?"

"I think I might have an idea where she may have gone. Pray deliver that note, and if I am right, I will bring Corliss to her cousin very soon."

Geoffrey started on his errand with a troubled mind. They had been good to Corliss, he thought, but there were what you might call undercurrents just out of sight. His experience with adults made him wary of the unreason that seemed to guide his elders in their wayward paths. He could not understand, nor did he think he ever wanted to. Life was much simpler if one did what one was told, and not try to understand it.

He walked quickly toward Portland Place.

Douglas was too late to take advantage of Charles's offer to share his hackney. Besides, if Charles were seeking Isabel, he would be moving in a direction different from that intended by Douglas.

It was a brisk walk to his destination, but a hackney in the carriage and cart traffic would be no swifter. Besides, Douglas wanted to test his theory.

She—Douglas did not need to speak a name, for there was only one "she"—must be miserably unhappy. All the family ructions exploding around her, the weeks of playing a part that oddly was not a part, could not help but take a toll on a delicately nurtured female. He wondered what the Garnetts had said in that morning room, unencumbered by Corliss's presence. They surely had spoken their minds freely, and it was the worst of bad luck that they had been overheard.

He could not even guess what she had heard, but that she was unhappy was evident. He had expected his courtship to run smoothly. He knew she liked him, and certainly he had made no secret of his feelings for her.

He had gone over that last afternoon with her, over every word that he could remember, to understand what had turned her against him. Somewhere during one of his many sleepless nights, he had remembered. What an idiot he had been!

To speak of honesty, of integrity, to a girl burdened with the secret of the plot that Isabel and Geoffrey had later laid bare before him, was the most abominable arrogance! Who was he to hold up standards for her? He had, although he did not like to dwell on it, bent a few canons himself.

Since he had not wished to embarrass her by personal remarks—her lapis lazuli eyes, her sweet, merry ways, her glossy dark ringlets, even her grace of movement—he had compromised by mentioning unexceptional virtues. Such as honesty.

If she were wretched, he believed she would seek solace by returning to a place where, once, for a brief time, she had been happy.

He found her where he expected her to be.

He hurried down Old Bond Street, passing by the entrance to St. James's Street, and entered the park by the small lane that ran beside Clarence House. He searched with a rising tightness in his chest, for if she were not here, then he did not know where else to look.

At last he caught sight of her. She stood uncertainly on the walk, near a small coppice of trees, almost to the circle and the Mall beyond. She looked lost, bewildered, at sea. Her forlorn posture wrenched at his heart.

He walked across the grass toward her. She

caught sight of him, and gladness leaped into her face. So he hadn't made a mistake, he thought. His great relief was the measure of the worry he had carried unconsciously with him.

She ran a few steps toward him, and he opened his arms and took her in.

They stood thus for a long time. Isabel and Charles, coming from the direction of the bridge, caught sight of them. Isabel would have cried out and rushed to the couple, but Charles held her back.

"This is their time, my dear."

The anxiousness with which Charles had found her, standing alone by the bridge, and the peal he rang over her when he saw she was unharmed, had induced in Isabel a state of well-being approaching bliss. Emboldened by a confidence she did not know she had, she said softly, "And when will our time be?"

"Minx!" he said fondly. "As soon as your mother can be persuaded. You're making a big mistake, you know. You are so young. There is so much ahead of you—all the gaiety of London."

"Pooh!" said Isabel inelegantly. "I think we're all not made for the fashionable life. I've played at being a parlor maid, Geoffrey makes a good footman. And look at those two. Nothing so scandalous as an embrace, in public!" But she was smiling, and, if truth be told, slightly envious.

In the middle of Green Park, the storm was of a different nature. Corliss did not cry, at least loudly. She was not even aware of the tears brimming from her dark blue eyes and slipping down her cheeks.

"How did you know I was here?"

"Because, my darling girl, I just knew."

"And you came after me?"

"Naturally. You belong to me, don't you know that?"

"Oh— But I must tell you—

"You must tell me nothing, dearest Corliss. Some day when we are too old to do anything but sit by the fire, I will hold your hand and you can tell me everything that happened to you before I met you."

"Douglas—"

"Now, hush. I am taking you to your family. Lady Dacre is expecting you, and I am sure she will agree to let you be married from her home."

"But there is my brother—"

"You may forget your brother, my dear, if you will. If I see much of him, I shall be forced to call him out. I do not expect he is a famous duellist?"

She laughed, a little gurgle in her throat that encouraged him greatly. "I am sure he meant well."

"I am not at all sure of that, but I bow to your greater knowledge of him. However, darling, darling Corliss, we have some unfinished business to take care of."

"I do not understand?"

"I was about to offer, last time we were here. Do you recall?"

"Oh, yes, Douglas. I was so happy to know that you cared a little for me!"

"A little?"

He tightened his embrace, and tilted her face up to his. They could have been on a desert isle, or in the middle of Piccadilly. He kissed her thoroughly. He looked seriously into her eyes, then, and what he saw there led him to repeat his scandalous behavior, to the great satisfaction of them both.

It was at this point that Charles took Isabel's arm and turned her toward Hanover Square. The interview to come with Mrs. Garnett might be stormy, but perhaps the turbulence might be lessened by the good news that Corliss had been found, safe.

It was worth a try!

ABOUT THE AUTHOR

Vanessa Gray grew up in Oak Park, Illinois, and graduated from the University of Chicago. She currently lives in the farm country of northeastern Indiana, where she pursues her interest in the history of Georgian England and the Middle Ages.